Dear Arthur,

I'm sorry I didn't show up for our wedding, but after Travis Blakeman showed me those...pictures of you, I had no other choice. In fact, knowing that you betrayed me before we even took our vows made me feel justified in getting out of a marriage that, I've known for some time, was bound to be a grave mistake.

As for how I left the church—well, jumping out the window seemed to be the only tactful way to handle it. But don't worry, I didn't hurt myself; in fact, that nice Mr. Blakeman managed to catch me in his arms just as I was about to hit the ground. So really, I'm fine.

As for where I am now, well, Travis—that is, Mr. Blakeman—offered me the use of his cabin for a few days to get myself together. I didn't think he was going to stay here with me, but it looks like he is. Well, I can certainly use the company....

At any rate, I'm sorry our wedding was a fiasco— but I know it's for the best. Have a nice life.

Sincerely,

Lucy

Please address questions and book requests to: Silhouette Reader Service
U.S.: 3010 Walden Ave., P.O. Box 1325, Buffalo, NY 14269
Canadian: P.O. Box 609, Fort Erie, Ont. L2A 5X3

Runaway Brides

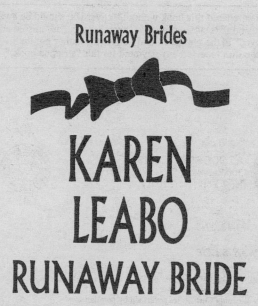

# KAREN LEABO
# RUNAWAY BRIDE

*Silhouette Books*

Published by Silhouette Books
**America's Publisher of Contemporary Romance**

SILHOUETTE BOOKS
300 East 42nd St.,
New York, N.Y. 10017

ISBN 0-373-30137-5

RUNAWAY BRIDE

## A Letter from the Author

Dear Reader,

Everyone loves a bride, and I have a special place in my heart for one in particular—Lucy Walker. Lucy stands out in my mind, I think, because I laughed the whole time I was writing about her adventures in *Runaway Bride*. Naturally, I was thrilled to learn that a whole new crop of readers will get to know her and Travis Blakeman, her knight in shining armor, via this reissue.

The idea for Lucy and her wedding predicament came to me when, in my mind's eye, I saw a bride jumping out a window and landing on top of the unsuspecting hero. At the time, I didn't know why she wanted so badly to escape matrimony. All I knew was that she was desperate enough to trust in a total stranger to carry her off. I had a fantastic time, too, figuring out what she was running from.

As for the bride herself, I decided no long-limbed, sophisticated blonde or sultry brunette would get herself in such a fix. Instead, Lucy turned out to be a short redhead who's painfully shy. She and Travis have to be the mismatch of the decade!

I hope you enjoy *Runaway Bride*, that it gives you a reason to smile. I also hope you'll enjoy the many other fine novels in the Silhouette Romance line, the line that started it all for Silhouette readers and launched me into the most fun career I can imagine.

All my best,

*Karen Leabo*

# Chapter One

Lucy Walker stared into the full-length mirror, scarcely believing that the creature she viewed was herself. Her face was pasty white, almost as white as the frothy satin-and-lace gown that encased her from her neck to the floor. Her mouth was a red slash, her eyes wide and too bright. Her straight hair had been tortured into fiery red ringlets, peeking out from an enormous nest of netting and seed pearls.

I must be the most hideous bride ever to walk the earth, she thought with a small shudder.

"She looks ravishing," her mother declared. "Look, girls, isn't she a vision?"

Her sisters' faces appeared on either side of Lucy in the mirror—identical images, swathed in turquoise taffeta. "Breathtaking," agreed Sandy, the oldest of the three sisters. "Henri did wonders with her hair."

"The dress is an absolute dream," said Judy, the youngest. "Are you wearing the heels, Luce?"

"I'm wearing them," Lucy assured her sister through tight lips. Three-and-a-half-inch satin stilts, and her feet were painfully aware of every inch. She could hardly stand in them, much less walk.

"Here, let's see how she looks holding her bouquet." Sandy thrust a gaudy mound of gardenias into Lucy's numb hands. The sickly sweet scent was almost overpowering.

Lucy's mother, Gwen, clapped her hands together in satisfaction. "Beautiful. Arthur will swoon, he'll just swoon!"

Arthur will take one look at me and bolt from the church, Lucy thought. That was one grim scenario her too-vivid imagination hadn't yet conjured, and she dwelled on it for several horrifying moments.

"For heaven's sake, Lucy, can't you smile?" Sandy asked indulgently as she fussed with the veil's mountain of netting. "I know you're a little nervous, but this is the happiest day of your life."

For their sake she forced a smile, which only made her red lips look more ghastly. This was not, by any stretch of the imagination, the happiest day of her life.

It wasn't that she didn't want to marry Arthur. But she desperately wished she could have talked her fiancé into an elopement. If she had, she'd already be settled cozily into Arthur's country house—baking bread, feeding the geese, going for long walks alone. Or with Arthur.

Unfortunately she was here, in the bride's room at St. Jude's Catholic Church, and in twenty minutes she would be walking down the aisle with five hundred plus pairs of eyes glued to her every move. Images of herself tripping, dropping the ring or fainting dead away plagued her.

"You look a little pale, honey," her mother said. Gwen Walker appeared perfect, as usual, in a lilac chiffon gown, her strawberry blond hair smoothed into a dignified twist.

*A little? Dracula's bride had more color.*

"I have something that will calm you down," Sandy offered. "I know you don't like to take tranquilizers, Lucy, but frankly your nerves are shot."

"I'll be fine," Lucy snapped. She took a deep breath. All she needed was to walk down the aisle in a drugged stupor. "What I'd really like is a few moments alone. Some peace and quiet to collect myself. Could you do that one thing for me, please?" Lord knew they hadn't listened to any of her other requests.

Gwen was the first to respond. "All right, dear. We still have twenty minutes, and you're as ready as you'll get. Come on, girls." She reached for the door.

"I don't know, Mother," Judy objected. "I think she's about to have an anxiety attack. She looks just like she did that time at school, when she had to recite that poem and she threw—"

"Judy, *please*," Sandy interrupted. "Lucy doesn't want to think about that!"

"I am not about to have an anxiety attack," Lucy objected shrilly, unable to hide her irritation any longer. She'd been dragged around, stuffed into a dress, poked and prodded, primped and powdered until she was heartily sick of the whole mess. "I know you mean well, but just get out, please. And stop talking about me like I can't hear you."

Gwen ushered the two bridesmaids out the door, throwing a worried glance over her shoulder at her middle daughter. "You *are* okay, aren't you?" she asked.

Not trusting her voice, Lucy nodded.

"Good. I'm sure everything will go just fine. There's no reason to worry. And please don't sit down," Gwen said as an afterthought. "I wouldn't want you to wrinkle that gorgeous satin." Then she closed the door behind her.

Lucy felt her tenuous control slipping away. She counted to ten, then burst into tears.

Terrific, she thought miserably as she sobbed away, now I'll have to walk down the aisle with a red, blotchy face. She hobbled over to where her purse sat on the floor and stooped to pluck a tissue from the interior, but standing up was too much effort. She sank onto the floor in a puddle of utter misery, not giving a hoot what she did to the damn dress.

*Please, don't let them hear me crying,* she prayed as she did her best to mop up the persistent tears without smearing her so-carefully applied makeup. And as long as she was praying, she decided to pray for an earthquake. A tornado. A terrorist attack. Anything to prevent her from walking down that aisle in front of all those people.

Travis Blakeman's dark blue Fiat took the corner at thirty miles per hour, tires squealing. He had fifteen minutes to get to St. Jude's, where he would probably make a spectacle of himself. Still, better him than his half-crazed client. This was the absolute last domestic-relations case he would take on, he vowed to himself. His law firm seldom handled divorces, but he'd accepted this case, with reservations, because Brian Haney was a friend.

Now all those reservations were being validated. Minutes earlier he'd received a hysterical call from Brian, who had just discovered that Arthur Sprague, his wife's lover, was getting married. Brian had been all set to swoop into the church and destroy the wedding by hurling accusations at Arthur. Such behavior would have landed Brian in jail, jeopardizing his already tenuous chance at getting custody of his children.

The only way Travis was able to dissuade Brian was to promise to take care of the matter himself. That's why he was on his way to St. Jude's. But he intended to handle things much more diplomatically than Brian would have, and he hoped to save a great deal of pain and embarrassment.

The church parking lot was packed. It was obviously a big wedding. That made things even more awkward. He had less than ten minutes left, so he double parked. He grabbed a large envelope and sprinted from his car to the church, ignoring the objections of the parking attendant.

Travis had never done anything this crazy in his life, and now probably wasn't a good time to start—not when he was preparing to launch a political campaign. His only hope was to accomplish his mission without drawing too much attention to himself.

He found a door with a plaque that read Bride's Room. That looked like a safe bet. No one seemed to notice him, so he tapped lightly on the door.

There was no answer. He started to tap again when he heard a faint, "Come in."

He turned the knob and stepped in cautiously. There, sitting on the floor, was the most abject-looking creature he'd ever seen. She appeared so tiny, so delicate. Only the flame-red hair prevented her from disappearing against the voluminous white dress. For a few moments, all he could do was stare at her.

She was crying, he realized with a jolt.

"Are you the bride?" he asked, then wanted to kick himself. Who the hell else could she be?'

"No, I'm Little Bo-Peep," she answered between sniffles. "Who are you and what do you want?"

His heart went out to her. She looked so tragic. Maybe she'd already learned of her fiancé's escapades.

"Listen," he said. "I know this is very awkward and I offer my sincerest apologies for intruding on such a . . . a . . . special occasion, but I thought you should know." He handed her the large white envelope.

"Know what?"

"The photos will explain everything. I'm really, really sorry, Miss—I don't even know your name."

"Lucy," she mumbled, opening the envelope and extracting the thick stack of eight-by-ten glossies.

He watched, concerned as to what the woman's reaction might be. She was already in a precarious emotional state. He'd hate to think he was responsible for causing her to faint or go completely hysterical, and with no one around to help her.

She did neither. In fact, she stopped crying altogether as she studied the photographs, her brow creased in angry furrows. "That two-timing son of a—Where did you get these?"

"They were taken by a private investigator about a month ago, in St. Louis. They're connected to a divorce case I'm handling." That was all she needed to know, he decided.

She eyed him thoughtfully. "Showing them to me was your good deed for the day, huh?"

"You can ignore them if you want. I can slip out of here and no one need be the wiser."

"Ignore them?" To his surprise, she smiled. "Mister, it seems prayers do get answered. You're not quite as good as an earthquake, but..." She shrugged. "This'll sure make a handy excuse for calling off a wedding."

"Didn't you want to get married?" he asked, confused.

She lowered her eyes. "I did, but this wedding...ah, it's too complicated to explain. Let's just say I don't want to marry him now."

"Good, I'm glad." He took the pictures. They represented evidence in an ongoing case, so he couldn't allow them to circulate. He'd already bent the rules a little by revealing this information outside the courtroom, though his client had given him permission.

With the envelope in hand he wished the little bride luck, then reluctantly left her. He managed to get out of the church unnoticed.

Lucy, still reeling from this shocking turn of events, couldn't decide what to do first. Instead of dealing with the problem at hand, her thoughts remained with her handsome benefactor. He was drop-dead gorgeous—no question about that—with thick, curly brown hair and whiskey-brown eyes to match. His khaki trousers and mint-green golf shirt were casual but expensive, and his tall, trim body suggested that he was at least a weekend athlete.

He hadn't offered his name, and she hadn't asked. Maybe it was better that way.

Oddly, her initial outrage over Arthur's betrayal had already dissipated somewhat. She had every reason to be downright hysterical about such a blatant betrayal, and yet . . . Doubtless she was simply too numb with shock to be upset. She'd worry about that later.

Right now, she had to figure out how to announce to five hundred people that the wedding was off. She grew queasy at the very thought.

She couldn't do it—she just couldn't.

She knew what would happen. She'd open her mouth, and no words would come out, and then the organist would start the processional, and before she knew it she'd be Mrs. Arthur Sprague.

Even if she did manage to make herself understood, she had no way of knowing how her family would react. Lucy had always been a bit fanciful—she herself admitted that—and her parents might assume she was overreacting to some inconsequential bit of gossip, or that she'd misunderstood altogether. They were very fond of Art, and they would have a hard time believing he could betray her. They might even try to persuade her to go through with the ceremony.

The whole thing was just too mortifying to even consider. No, she couldn't face them. She had just one option, and that was escape. She'd have to hurry, too, because the wedding was about to begin.

She scrawled a hasty note on a piece of church stationery. When her mother and sisters came to get her, they would find only the note. Then *they* would have to make all those awkward explanations to the five hundred guests. That thought made her smile, though briefly.

Kicking off the killer heels, she grabbed the jeans, T-shirt and loafers she'd worn to the church. She dragged a chair to the window, unlatched and opened it and threw her bundle of clothing out. Then she attempted to climb up and over the sill.

The billowing skirts hampered her efforts, and the veil wanted to wrap itself across her face. With the satin bunched around her thighs, she finally got herself poised for the jump. But when she pushed the netting out of her eyes and looked down, she gasped. It was a long way to the ground.

Maybe she'd better lower herself slowly. She turned and grabbed the sill with her hands, then eased her body down the brick wall until she was dangling. She held her breath and prepared to let go.

"What the hell are you doing?" a voice called up to her.

"Escaping," she called back. It was him, the man with the pictures. She couldn't see him, but she recognized his voice. Her arms were starting to ache.

"Don't let go," he cautioned. "It's too far. You'll hurt yourself."

She was about to decide the same thing. But she couldn't pull herself up. The muscles in her arms were on fire. "I don't have any choice. I'm slipping."

"I'll try to catch you," he said, just as her fingers slid loose from the sill.

She fell like a bag of wet cement, right on top of the poor man. They thudded to the ground in a tangle of arms, legs, and white satin.

"Are you okay?" she asked as she pulled herself and her dress free of him. "You shouldn't have stood underneath me that way. I might have broken your neck."

"You might have broken yours," he shot back as he sat up, rubbing his elbow. "Just what are you trying to prove?"

"I'm not trying to prove anything. I told you, I'm escaping. Would you like to aid and abet me in my crime?"

"No!" he answered without hesitation. Had he actually thought this virago was fragile, delicate?

"Then I'm outta here. Thanks for breaking my fall." She stood and slipped her stockinged feet into penny loafers as she gathered up the clothing that had preceded her out the window. Then she marched away from the church, head held high, though her dress bore grass stains and her head-piece was askew.

He pushed himself up and trotted after her. "Wait, where are you going?"

"First, away from here. I'll figure the rest out later."

"But you can't go traipsing around downtown Brennerton in a wedding dress," he objected.

"Watch me."

The poor thing was unhinged, he decided. The shock of her fiancé's deception had been too much for her. He ran to his car, which he'd abandoned **on** the edge of the parking lot when he'd seen that bundle of clothes fly out the window and had gone to investigate. He pulled up ahead of her and opened the passenger door from the inside. "Hop in," he called. "I'll take you home."

She shot him a grateful smile and piled into his small car, pulling yards of white satin in with her before slamming the door. The sheer volume of whiteness was overpowering, and Travis found himself pushing the netting of her veil out of his face.

"I'll take you home if you'll answer one question," he amended once the car was moving again. "Why didn't you just call off the wedding, instead of risking your life crawling out a window?"

Her face seemed to lose what little color it had regained. "I couldn't call it off."

"Why not? I'm sure it wouldn't have been pleasant, but—"

"It's not a case of wishing to avoid an unpleasant scene. I was really afraid I wouldn't be able to stop the wedding, that I'd have been hustled through that ceremony faster than I could blink twice."

"Aren't you being a little melodramatic?" he asked. "I mean, no woman in this day and age can be forced to marry against her wishes."

"If she makes her wishes known," Lucy countered. "In my case it's doubtful I could have. My tongue would have frozen to the roof of my mouth. I'm, uh, not a strong public speaker, especially when I'm nervous to begin with.''

"Too bad I couldn't have left the pictures with you. They speak volumes,'' he said.

"Even if you had, they might have been ignored or explained away. The wedding was already like a locomotive out of control. I just wasn't sure I could stop it no matter what I said or did, and after I saw those photos I knew I couldn't marry Arthur. Who are you, anyway?'' she asked.

"Travis Blakeman.'' Automatically he held out a hand to her. She shook it with a firm grip. "Why were you crying when I first came into that room?'' he asked impulsively.

"You said just one question,'' she reminded him.

He nodded. She was no dummy. "All right. Tell me where you live, and I'll take you there.''

She was silent for a moment. "I don't have a home,'' she said, as if that realization had just dawned on her. "All my stuff has been moved to Arthur's, and I sublet my apartment to my little sister and her husband. They've already moved in.''

"Can I take you to your parents' place, then?''

"No,'' she answered, visibly recoiling. "I'm not ready to face them and their questions. They won't understand. You can take me to a hotel, I guess.''

"Ah, I know just the place.''

A few minutes later, as Travis headed the Fiat onto the highway, Lucy asked, "How far is it?"

"About twenty minutes. My sister owns a peaceful little resort on Taluka Lake. I thought you might like someplace quiet to sort things out." And Nan could keep an eye on her in the meantime, he added to himself.

Lucy nodded her acquiescence. As her adrenaline level dropped, the enormity of what she had done sank in and she lapsed into silence. Her stunt was bound to make the local paper. The residents of Brennerton, Missouri, loved a good scandal, and what could be more scandalous than a state legislator's daughter skipping out on her own wedding?

Her father would not appreciate the embarrassing publicity she'd invited upon the family.

"Second thoughts?" Travis asked. "I can still take you back, if you want."

She made a face. "No way. I was just wishing that I'd had the nerve to face Arthur, that's all—instead of sneaking away."

"Funny, you don't seem the timid type to me."

"Really?" She stopped to ponder this, and realized that she had indeed been carrying on a bona fide conversation with a complete stranger, something that didn't happen very often. In fact, there weren't too many people in the world who didn't reduce her to silence. She'd learned the habit as a very young child, when a troublesome stutter had made talking an excruciating experience. Though she'd long since left the speech impediment behind, she'd never overcome her shyness.

"I know we just met," Travis said, "but you seem about as shy and retiring as a freight train."

"I guess I was just so shocked I forgot to be shy." She found herself laughing. "I can't imagine what you must think of me—sobbing like a five-year-old one minute, jumping out a window the next."

"In all honesty, I don't quite know what to think of you, Lucy." He said this with humor, so she wasn't in the least bit offended.

"Normally I'm not quite so... overdramatic. I lead a very peaceful existence."

"I'll bet."

"No, really," she protested as his smile grew wider. He had a nice smile, she conceded. A friendly one, despite his teasing. From her side of the car she could only see him in profile, but she noticed the dimple at the right corner of his mouth, and she wondered if he had a matching one on the other side.

Lucy sensed that until he knew her better, he wouldn't believe that she was shy, so she didn't bother to argue. She certainly hadn't shown that side of herself to him, which still amazed her. He simply did not make her nervous.

Arthur had put her at ease, too, she mused, though she couldn't recall talking such a blue streak with him. For one thing, he talked a lot himself. He was a fascinating man, having traveled all over the world with his father, an international wheeler-dealer.

Lucy had been taken with Art from the moment her father had invited him to a family dinner two years ago, a none-too-subtle matchmaking effort that both of them had caught on to. She had been enthralled with his amusing anecdotes, the diversity of his education, the places he'd lived. His fair good looks hadn't hurt, either.

She sighed. *Face it, Lucy, your one and only prospect for marriage is down the tubes.* She braced herself for the tears to return. They didn't. She decided she must still be in shock.

Travis had turned off the highway a few minutes earlier and was threading his way down a narrow, winding road flanked by lush woodlands. The weather was unseasonably warm, even for July, and the Fiat's air-conditioning left much to be desired. Lucy cracked her window for a breath of fresh air. The breeze played havoc with her billowy veil, though it didn't so much as ruffle her cast-iron hairstyle.

"Not much farther," Travis said, as if sensing her antsiness. True to his word, they soon turned down a bumpy dirt road that twisted through the majestic trees. At the top of a rise Lucy could glimpse Taluka Lake, a gleaming gem in the dark green landscape. Late-afternoon sunlight sprinkled through the leaves, highlighting the small motel that was to be her temporary refuge.

Hide-Away Lodge, the weather-beaten sign announced. "What an appropriate name," she said, and Travis laughed. She took inordinate pleasure in the fact that she *could* make him laugh, even if she hadn't really been trying.

The moment he'd brought the car to a halt, Travis leaped out and ran around to the passenger side to help Lucy. She was already in trouble, struggling to free her feet from the sea of white puffiness.

"I should have dispensed with these petticoats first thing," she said as he assisted her out of the car, then retrieved her bundle of clothes and handed them to her. "What a nuisance. I don't know how Scarlett O'Hara could stand them."

"Scarlett O'Hara never rode in a compact sports car," he said.

"Good point." She gathered up the train and started toward a porch, which shadowed the entrance to the rustic motel. Two hand-carved wooden geese adorned the front door, proclaiming a message of welcome, and a cheery jangle of bells announcing the new arrivals.

Once inside Lucy paused, her nerves fluttering wildly. "What are we going to say?" she asked.

"We're going to ask my sister to give you a room for the night," Travis replied.

"But I'm wearing a wedding dress. Won't your sister ask questions?"

"I'm sure Nan will be very discreet," he said, just as a woman's booming voice assaulted them from across the room.

"Travis, my gracious, is that you?" A huge woman had just emerged from the back room and was bulldozing her way toward them. She looked to be almost as tall as Travis, who was over six feet, and she definitely outweighed him. She had fly-away blond hair, and a broad, square face. If this was Travis's sister, Lucy thought, she didn't look a thing like him.

As the woman caught sight of Lucy she skidded to a halt. "Good Lord, Travis, you went and got married without telling me!"

"No, no," he explained hastily. "She's not my bride. She's, um, someone else's."

"Well for goodness sake, who does she belong to and what is she doing with you?"

Travis turned to introduce Lucy, and realized she'd taken a couple of steps back until she was almost behind him. He touched her shoulder and urged her forward. "Lucy, meet my sister, Nan Blakeman."

Lucy hesitated before extending her hand toward Nan's outstretched one, and Travis caught a glimpse of the timid woman Lucy claimed to be. "Pleased to meet you," she said in almost a whisper, snatching her hand back and casting her eyes to the floor.

Nan was at once enchanted by her, as Travis had known she would be. Despite her blustery demeanor, his older sister was a sucker for strays. She leaned down a few inches, to be closer to Lucy's level. "Did something go wrong, honey?"

Lucy said nothing, but she looked at Travis with huge green eyes, silently beseeching him to bail her out.

"Save the questions for later, okay?" he asked Nan. "She needs a room for the night, and she could probably use a good, hot meal, too."

"Sure, no problem," Nan replied with a toothy smile. "I have lots of vacancies, unfortunately." She hustled behind the registration desk and produced a fat guest book. "If you'll just sign here—" She stopped when she saw the slight negative shake of Travis's head. "No, never mind, we can do the paperwork later. I'll bet you're just dying to get out of that hot dress. Come this way, and I'll show you to your cabin."

Lucy nodded, and the three of them made a procession out the front door, through the parking lot and down a footpath that followed a line of pseudo log cabins. The Hide-Away Lodge had been built in the fifties, but Nan had done a creditable job of giving the place a more historic feel.

Nan took them to the last cabin in the row. "This one's nice and private," she said as she opened the front door. It was warm and stuffy inside, but as soon as she had turned on the light she flipped the switch of a window air-conditioning unit. "Should cool off shortly. Seating for dinner starts at six-thirty—baked Virginia ham and redeye gravy, mashed potatoes, spinach and peach cobbler. I'll see you in a bit, now." She bustled out, leaving Travis and Lucy alone in the small room.

With a sigh Lucy threw her purse and her bundle of clothes onto the double bed, then began pulling the pins out of her elaborate headpiece. "She's right, you know. This dress is unmercifully hot."

Travis leaned against the door, arms folded over his chest, and studied her for a moment without comment. From the moment Nan had come on the scene, Lucy had seemed a different person—withdrawn, tongue-tied, awkward, even. Yet now she appeared completely at ease again.

"You really are shy, aren't you?" he questioned at last.

"I told you I was." She yanked the headpiece free of her corkscrew-curled red hair, then began working at the row of buttons down the back of her dress. "I guess I should have asked your sister to help me with these."

"You barely said a single word to her."

"I know. I'm sorry."

"There's no need to apologize. I wasn't criticizing. I'm just amazed, that's all. I know Nan is big and loud, but she's a sweet, generous lady, believe me."

"Oh, I'm sure she is," Lucy agreed. "I like her, just from the little I saw of her. Oh, these damn buttons! I've got to get out of this dress."

"I'll get them," he offered.

She hesitated, then turned her back to him, and he began working at the endless row of satin-covered buttons. His hands felt clumsy, and clumsier still the longer he worked. As each stubborn fastening came loose, more and more of Lucy's bare back was revealed, and more of Travis's composure faltered.

Until now he'd thought of her as more of a child bride or a china doll. Now he could see what the frothy dress had hidden—a slender body that tapered down to a tiny waist and lusciously flared hips, clearly proclaiming Lucy a full-grown woman despite her petite stature.

His hands were shaking a bit by the time he finished the task. "All done."

"Thanks."

"Need anything else before I go?" he asked.

She couldn't think of a thing, except maybe a one-way ticket to Siberia, which was about as far as she'd have to go to escape the repercussions of her mad dash for freedom. "I think I'm set, for now.

You've been a peach, Travis. I can't thank you enough for being so chivalrous."

He shrugged. "I guess chivalry is hard to come by in this day and age. Glad I could be of service." He started to leave, paused, then turned to her with a mischievous grin.

He only had the one dimple, she noticed. Before that thought had even registered, he'd taken two steps toward her. He leaned down and kissed her, so quickly she had no time to even think about stopping him. It was a mere brushing of his lips to hers.

"Just wanted to kiss the bride," he said, grinning wickedly. She was still staring after him, clutching her sagging dress to her body, as he whisked himself out the door.

# Chapter Two

Travis could have cheerfully run over himself with his own car. "That was a damn stupid stunt," he muttered as he walked toward the motel parking lot. What had possessed him?

The last thing that poor girl needed was kissing. She had enough to think about without having to fend off some guy who thought he was Sir Lancelot, demanding payment of a kiss for rescuing the damsel in distress.

Of course, she hadn't done much fending, he thought, smiling despite himself. When he'd come toward her, she'd reflexively turned her face upward and closed her eyes, as if to welcome him. Originally he'd planned to just peck her on the forehead. The decision to touch his lips to hers had been a split-second impulse.

Remembering that instantaneous contact made his lips tingle, then his whole body. "Stupid stunt," he muttered again, shaking his head.

Well, no use dwelling on it. He would soon be out of her life. He glanced at his watch and frowned. If he didn't get a move on, he'd be late for his tennis game.

He paused by his car. Thinking of Lucy, he realized he didn't want to abandon her like this. What if she didn't have any money with her? Nan would no doubt let her get away without paying; that was the kind of person his sister was. But she could scarcely afford to house and feed guests at no charge. The Hide-Away Lodge was suffering through one its slowest summers ever.

Travis decided to pay for Lucy's room and dinner himself, just to be sure. He'd leave his home phone number for her, too, in case she needed something. With his conscience soothed, he loped toward the office.

Nan sat at the front desk wearing a set of headphones, her nose buried in the Saturday paper. She looked up and gave him a wily smile when the doorbell announced his entrance. "You've done some dumb things in your life, Trav, but this one takes the cake," she said, pulling off the earphones. "Your little bride-napping stunt made the news."

"*What?*"

"I just heard it on the radio. Your fugitive bride has the whole town talking. What exactly *did* you do to break up the wedding?"

Quelling his unease, he explained, as best he could, the circumstances leading to his escorting the cold-footed bride to Nan's motel.

Nan tried, and failed, to control her laughter.

"This isn't funny," he insisted. "I just hope my name stays out of it. Arthur Sprague's family is prominent, but who would have guessed they could turn his wedding into a media event?"

Nan rolled her eyes. "It's not his family, idiot, it's hers. And I wouldn't count on staying anonymous if I were you."

"Hers? Lucy's? Who is she?"

"You mean you don't know?"

Travis shook his head numbly. He had a feeling he was about to find out.

"She's Lucy Walker. Daughter of none other than our illustrious state representative, Leon Walker. The man whose political support you were counting on, right?"

Travis's head spun for a moment. How had her identity escaped his attention? He was usually so meticulous about details. Then again, he'd been in a hell of a rush this afternoon, intent on reaching the church before the wedding could take place.

His embryonic bid for the mayor's office appeared doomed. He had practically kidnapped a state legislator's daughter, after all, and destroyed a multi-thousand-dollar wedding. Never mind how noble his intentions were.

Unless... "Maybe no one at the church saw me," he said. Then he remembered the parking attendant, and his hopes waned again.

"Lucy saw you," Nan pointed out. "Do you think she'll keep quiet about all this?"

Travis thought for a moment. "She might at that," he said, recalling all she'd told him about her shyness. "Besides, she's grateful to me for saving her from marrying that creep Arthur. She wouldn't deliberately turn the incident against me. Just the same, I suppose I'd better stick around and have a talk with her. Can I stay for dinner?"

"It'll cost you six ninety-five." Nan flashed him an impish grin that reminded him of the pretty, flirtatious young woman she'd once been.

She was his half-sister, actually, his father's daughter by a previous marriage, and thirteen years older than Travis. The two children hadn't been raised in the same household, but always had an affinity for one another. They'd grown closer as Travis had struggled into adulthood, searching for an identity apart from their wealthy father.

"Don't worry, I'll pay for my dinner," he assured her. "I'd like to pay for Lucy's dinner and her room, too."

"Better pay it in cash," Nan teased. "Just think what a reporter could do if he came across that credit card receipt."

Travis laughed, but the thought gave him a chill. Thus far he hadn't warranted any sort of attention from reporters. The only time his name had gotten into print was when he had made partner at the medium-size Brennerton law firm where he'd worked ever since passing the bar. But the moment he announced his candidacy it would be open season. The press would scrutinize his past, probably more carefully than his stand on the issues.

His record, both professional and personal, was scrupulously clean. Reporters could dig until their shovels broke, and they wouldn't find a single embarrassing episode in his past.

Until now.

Much as he hated to, he called to cancel his tennis date. His partner, a young city council member, was easily insulted, and Travis needed the man's support, but his current dilemma was more urgent.

Ah, well, he'd deal with that later, he thought as he helped Nan in the huge motel kitchen, mashing potatoes and loading them with more butter than he knew was healthy. But the motel guests didn't patronize Nan's dining room for nouvelle cuisine.

They came here to eat hearty, and Nan prided herself on the fact that they never went away hungry.

When most of the cooking was done, well ahead of schedule, Nan shooed Travis out of the kitchen and told him to help Wanda, a local teenager who waited and bussed tables. But Wanda had everything under control in the dining room, so he took a seat at a booth by the window and browsed through an area tourism guide.

The guests trickled in, in twos and threes. Most of those who stayed at the Hide-Away Lodge were regulars. Nan, having changed from her jeans into a flattering denim jumper, greeted the old-timers by name and made the newcomers feel right at home.

Without turning around, Travis knew when Lucy entered the dining room. Perhaps it was the sound of the door opening tentatively, then closing so quietly, or the softness of her footsteps on the linoleum floor. Or maybe it was her subtle baby powder scent, which reached him just moments before Nan showed her to his table.

If Lucy was surprised to see him still there, he was equally surprised at her appearance. She hardly resembled the tragic little bride she'd been earlier. Gone were the Shirley Temple ringlets and the smudged makeup. Her shoulder-length hair was water straight, a curtain of fire that hung just to her shoulders. It was still damp from her recent bath. A row of impudent bangs, which should have made her look young, instead added a stylish splash to her appearance.

Her softly faded jeans emphasized her pleasingly curved hips and the Tulane University T-shirt hugged her full breasts in all the right places.

"I thought you'd be long gone," she said, taking a seat on the other side of the booth. She looked everywhere but at him.

She was remembering that kiss, that silly kiss, he was sure of it. He should apologize, but talking about it would likely make her more uncomfortable. The best thing to do was pretend it had never happened.

"I felt bad about leaving you here all alone, on your wedding day and all," he confessed. "Besides, there's something I want to ask you."

Wanda chose that moment to bring heaping plates to their table. "Can I get you something to drink?" she asked.

Since Lucy seemed indecisive, Travis answered for both of them. "Bring us a couple of Cokes."

She looked at him in surprise. "I could have ordered my own drink," she said when Wanda had left. "I'm not mute."

"Would you have preferred iced tea?" he asked, taking the reprimand in stride.

She sighed. "No, soda's fine. Guess I'm just tired of people making decisions for me."

"That tends to happen when you don't make decisions for yourself," he said.

"I make decisions," she argued. "I just don't always make them real fast or real loud."

Wanda brought their drinks, and for a few moments they concentrated on Nan's succulent ham. Lucy demolished half of what was on her plate before speaking again. "You said you had something to ask me?"

"Oh, right. It seems we created quite a stir by breaking up your wedding."

"Hmm, I'm not surprised. Dad's probably called out the National Guard to track me down."

"Doesn't that worry you?"

She shrugged. "I doubt they'd look for me here. Besides, I'll call my parents in a bit and let them know I'm okay, and that I haven't taken leave of my senses. I left a note behind, but I'm afraid it didn't explain much."

"I'm glad you didn't marry that guy," he said, and he really meant it.

"It would have been a mistake, I suppose."

"You don't seem too upset," he ventured. "In fact, I get the distinct impression that you're... relieved?"

She squirmed uncomfortably at his question. "I should be more upset than I am," she agreed. "At first I thought I was too shocked to feel much of anything. But now that it's had a chance to sink in,

I'm just . . . well, I guess I am relieved that the wedding ordeal is over. I'll never do that again.''

"Never get married?" he asked, eyebrows raised.

"If I do, I'll elope," she quipped.

"Did you love him?" he asked gently.

She let a sigh escape. "Right now, I'd like to have him drawn and quartered. But yes, I did love him. Or I thought I did, anyway," she added in an undertone.

"Why?" he asked, before he could stop himself.

She glared at him. "Because I'm an idiot? Is that what you're getting at?"

*Way to go, Blakeman,* he congratulated himself. He'd offended her. Not a smart thing to do when he had to turn around and ask for her cooperation.

"That was rude of me," he said. "I'm not normally so lacking in tact."

"Can we change the subject?" she asked coolly.

"Yes, of course. There is something else I wanted to ask you. What I did today—ruining your wedding—has put me in a very delicate situation."

"Couldn't be as bad as the one I'm in," she muttered, toying with the last of her mashed potatoes.

"You see, when my client called me to tell me he intended to bash up Arthur Sprague's wedding, I didn't press him for details. I just went into action, to prevent the man from creating a terrible scene and embarrassing everyone involved, including himself. I never dreamed that the woman Sprague intended to marry was—"

She stopped playing with her potatoes and was staring at him intently with large green eyes that made it hard for him to concentrate.

"You see, your father . . . well, I intend to . . ."

"You didn't know I was Leon Walker's daughter?" she supplied.

He nodded. "Exactly."

"I doubt he can do anything to you—he doesn't hold your mortgage, does he?"

"Nothing so mundane as that. But soon I'm planning to announce my bid for mayor, and I was hoping to get your father's support." There, he'd said it.

Lucy's mouth dropped open. "Wendall Cox has run unopposed for four terms," she finally managed. "And my father has always been one of his staunchest supporters."

"I'm aware of that. Look, I'm not asking you to support my decision to run. All I'm asking is that you be discreet about my part in your bolt for freedom. I wouldn't want you to lie about it, of course," he added, "but, well, you understand the position I'm in."

"Oh," she said, nodding. "If Dad finds out what you did, you'll be in quite a pickle."

"If *anyone* finds out," he clarified.

"You should understand that I love politics...but not politicians. I like nothing better than to see one of your kind embarrassed."

"How encouraging," he muttered.

"On the other hand, I'm delighted that someone finally has the guts to oppose Cox. He's grown quite complacent, and he's not doing much for the town. Dad is disgusted with him over the annexation issue." She set her chin in her hand and gazed thoughtfully at Travis.

He tried to keep from squirming. He was at her mercy, and she realized that fully.

"Tell me, Travis," she said. "If you had known who I was, would you have done what you did today?"

He thought about that for a moment. "I wish I could say yes," he answered honestly. "But I'm not sure. I might very well have chickened out, once I realized the political ramifications. I'm not usually prone to such impulsiveness."

"So you might have considered your political future first, and my unfortunate plight second," she clarified.

Much as he hated to, he nodded.

She smiled. "I like your honesty, Travis Blakeman. It'll probably ruin you for politics. Honest guys have it tough, sometimes." She paused and stared at him some more, as if sizing him up. "You might just give ol' Wendall a run for his money, and that's something I'd very much like to see. So yes, I'll be discreet. You did me a service, and you don't deserve to have your campaign tainted by your good deed.''

He allowed himself to breathe again. ''Thank you, Lucy.''

''How do you plan to defeat him?''

The question took him by surprise, and the glib answer he sought simply wasn't there.

''Come on, now, you'll have to do better than that with the reporters,'' she said.

''The issues,'' he finally managed. ''I've researched Cox's record thoroughly. He's a smart man, but he's more of a politician than a leader. He waffles on the issues, changing his stand whenever it's politically expedient. Take this annexation issue, for instance. He's already changed his mind about it twice. I think that by pointing out the inconsistencies in his record, and by taking a strong stand on some crucial points, like annexation, I can sway the voters,'' he concluded, feeling pleased with himself.

But Lucy was shaking her head. ''It's not enough.''

''No?''

''Cox has the support of the good-ol'-boy network. He has more people in this town who owe him more favors than you can shake a stick at. Trust me, Travis, you're going to have to penetrate that network. And you're going to have to get down in the trenches and play dirty if you want to defeat an incumbent mayor.''

''I don't play dirty,'' Travis said evenly.

''I'm not saying you have to be a slimeball. But you'd better be prepared to fight fire with fire.''

Her warning gave him a lot to think about. She had a valid point, one he didn't like to be reminded of. While his family wasn't completely without influence in these parts, Travis was not privy to the inner sanctum of old money and conservatism that Wendall Cox and Leon Walker occupied with ease. Travis was assured popularity among the younger movers and shakers, though; some of them were the children of old money.

Wanda brought two dishes of steaming peach cobbler with ice cream to the table, and for a few minutes Travis and Lucy indulged themselves.

''So what are your plans?'' Travis asked, handily changing the subject. It seemed a shame to waste an evening with a woman like Lucy talking about politics.

''I imagine I'll spend some time returning wedding gifts and doing a lot of uncomfortable explaining,'' she answered practically.

''It's Arthur who should have to explain,'' Travis said under his breath.

"And I'll have to find a place to live," she continued, ignoring his comment. "I've been wanting to move out of town anyway."

"Out of town?"

"To the country," she clarified. "My little carriage house apartment was so small I couldn't have any pets. I want some animals—chickens, maybe, or geese. Or a couple of goats. No, a pony! I've always wanted a pony," she said dreamily.

"I know just the place," he said, indulging her fantasy. "There's a little gingerbread house for sale just off Highway 7, in the hills north of town. According to the for-sale sign, it comes with twenty-two wooded acres and its own little lake."

"I've seen it," she said, nodding enthusiastically. It was the first time he'd seen her smiling and relaxed, and he liked it. "It's been on the market forever," she added.

"Maybe the owner doesn't really want to sell," Travis speculated. "It's such a pretty house."

"It probably has a pretty price tag to match." She sighed. "Well, it was a nice thought, but it sounds a bit out of my league."

*Out of her league?* He'd have thought Leon Walker's daughter could afford anything she wanted.

"There'll be no help from dear old Dad," she said, obviously guessing the direction of his thoughts. "He hasn't contributed to my support since college. After what I did today he'll probably cut me out of his will, too," she added dryly.

"There's that possibility," Travis said with a sage nod. His father had threatened it often enough. "Rich parents aren't always the blessing people think."

"Oh? And who's financing your political campaign?"

"My supporters," he answered without hesitation. "Mom and Dad are a little wishy-washy about my bid for office. They kinda like Wendall."

"Still, everyone knows you have to have family money behind you to run for office," she said. He would have thought the comment snide if he hadn't seen the mischief shining in her eyes.

"And I think we've asked each other enough impertinent questions," he countered. "Are you done with that?" He pointed to her half-empty plate of cobbler.

She pushed it toward him. "Be my guest. I'm stuffed."

He did. He never could resist Nan's baked goods.

"Better enjoy it while you can," Lucy said. "Soon it'll be nothing but rubber-chicken dinners for you. Frankly I don't understand why anyone would run for office."

"It's not something I'm doing for personal gratification, believe me."

"Why, then?"

That was a question he hadn't ever answered adequately, even to himself. "I feel compelled, I guess. I'm in a position to maybe make a difference, and I have to try."

She shook her head almost sadly. "So noble," she remarked. "I hope you know what you're doing."

"I don't, yet, but I'm learning."

Travis paid for their meal while Lucy used the pay phone to make the dreaded call to her parents. Her mother answered, but Leon immediately picked up an extension.

"Lucy, baby, where in heaven's name are you?" he demanded, sounding more worried than angry, which only added to Lucy's guilt. The family worried too much about her as it was.

"I'm staying at a hotel, and I'm safe," she assured them, despite the fact that her vocal cords were trying to close up on her.

"A hotel? Sweetheart, there's no need for you to hide out like that," he said. "Why don't you let your mother come pick you up and bring you home? Things aren't as bad as you think. I've circulated a story that you were ill. Art is here with us, and he's still willing to marry you. Father Michael is standing by—"

"Dad, hold on," she said, but her voice was too quiet to override his more strident one.

"You can still be married this evening, and no one need know you got cold feet. It'll be just the family this time—no crowds, no photographers...." When he finally paused, Lucy jumped in quickly.

"I'm not marrying Arthur," she said, surprised at the strength she put into the statement.

"You're what?" Gwen said in a choked voice.

"I'm not marrying Art," she repeated, though she was too mortified to tell them why, to admit that he'd been making a fool of her for who knows how long.

"That's preposterous," Leon blustered, unaccustomed to his middle daughter thwarting his wishes.

"It's not, really," Lucy said patiently.

"But why not?" Gwen broke in, starting to sob. "I don't understand."

"Ask Arthur," Lucy said miserably, though she doubted Art would supply the truth. No matter what fabrication he chose to tell them, he'd take great pains to stay in their good graces.

She heard her father's voice in the background. "Here, Art, you talk to her." And then, a moment later, Arthur's voice, smooth as heavy cream.

"Lucy, darling, I've been so worried. I—"

"Just be quiet for once, Arthur, and listen. Does the Bella Vista Motel ring a bell? I saw pictures of you there with that blond woman, so don't bother to deny it."

His tone changed abruptly, from heavy cream to broken glass. "We weren't married yet, you know. You can't have expected me to be a monk."

"I can and did expect you to be faithful."

"Look, darling, we can talk about this, all right?" He changed from broken glass to an out-of-tune violin.

"No, it's not all right." She took a deep breath. "We're not getting married, and that's final. I only wish I'd found out sooner, so I could have called off the wedding." At that point she decided she'd said all she needed to. "I have to go now. Tell Mother and Dad I'm sorry to waste such a ... *nice* wedding, and I'll be in touch."

"You can't do this to me, you know." The violin now sounded more like a cello, heavy and ominous. "I'll give you just one week to come to your senses."

*And do what?* She wanted to laugh at his ultimatum, but her lungs wouldn't cooperate. That pompous, arrogant little snipe! Since she couldn't summon an appropriate verbal response, she hung up the phone in his ear.

She turned and was surprised to find Travis standing right behind her. He put a steadying hand on her shoulder to keep them from colliding.

"Mission accomplished?" he asked.

"Uh-huh. The folks think I'm a little crazy. All in the world they've ever wanted was to see me happily married off, and now I've blown my big chance."

"Did you talk to Arthur?" Travis asked.

She nodded and rolled her eyes. "Arthur believes I should be more understanding, as if the strain of celibacy before our wedding was too much for any man to endure." She felt the blood rushing to her face as she realized what she'd just admitted. She had heard it was once again fashionable to be celibate before marriage, though fashion had little to do with why she hadn't gone to bed with Arthur. "Still," she continued hurriedly, "I think I made myself clear."

Without any spoken agreement, she and Travis left the dining room together and walked outside. The night was warm and clear, with just the hint of a breeze rustling through the leaves of the ancient oaks surrounding the motel. A full moon clearly illuminated their path.

"They say a full moon makes people do crazy things," Lucy said when they'd reached the small pier that jutted out onto the water of Taluka Lake. "Maybe that's what got into us today." She was at least half serious. Climbing out a window in a wedding dress, hitching a ride out of town with a complete stranger . . . letting that complete stranger kiss her. Today had to be the craziest day of her life.

She thought back to that stunned moment in the motel cabin when Travis had brushed his lips against hers. It had happened so swiftly she almost could have imagined it, except that the memory was much too vivid to have come from imagination alone.

Unconsciously she touched her hand to her lips as she and Travis stood side by side, gazing out over the water. Somewhere in the distance she heard the rustle of wings and the drowsy chirps of a water bird.

Desire. She recognized it, though she'd never felt it heat her blood in such a strange way before. She wasn't completely lacking in sexual experience. She'd done a bit of experimentation when she was away at college, where she'd felt more anonymous and less inhibited than in her hometown. But those few liaisons had left her flat compared to the feeling produced by the mere memory of Travis's innocent kiss.

As for Art...his warm, comfortable kisses hadn't seemed to lead anywhere. She'd never felt swept away, and he'd never pressed her.

"My God, I was going to settle for comfortable," she said.

"What?"

She was surprised that she'd spoken her thoughts aloud. "Oh, nothing much. I just realized that I was marrying Art for all the wrong reasons. He put me at ease. He made me feel comfortable. Those are *stupid* reasons to marry someone."

Travis made no response to that, except to slip his arm around her waist. He put her at ease, too, and she was attracted to him. Were the same unreliable forces at work?

"You don't have to stay," she said after another long silence. "I'll be fine, really. I promise not to throw myself into the lake in a fit of despair." She ducked away from his unsettling touch and sat on the end of the pier, dangling her legs over the water.

Travis joined her, despite her lack of an invitation. "I'd like to stay."

"Why?" she asked bluntly.

He hesitated. "I enjoy your company, that's all."

Oh, how she wanted to respond to that light flirtation. But she had no business trusting her emotions, not on a day like today.

"Do you want me to go?" he asked when she said nothing.

"No," she said against her better judgment. She even hoped he might kiss her again—really kiss her. She wanted to feel his mouth on hers, his tongue against hers. A perfectly crazy end to the day.

He disappointed her, because he made no move to take her in his arms. "You must be exhausted," he said as he hoisted himself to his feet. "I'd better hit the road and let you get some sleep."

She shook her head, trying to dispel the sensuous images that assaulted her. In the time it took her to do that, he disappeared.

## Chapter Three

"I really appreciate the ride," Lucy said from the passenger seat of Nan Blakeman's station wagon. They had just pulled up to the wrought-iron gates guarding the Walker estate. After sharing breakfast with Nan and then a ride into town, Lucy was gradually growing accustomed to the woman's overt friendliness, though she was still far from comfortable.

"It was no problem," Nan assured her as she put the car in neutral, then got out to unlock the tailgate. As Lucy retrieved her wadded-up dress and veil from the back, Nan gave a low whistle. "So, this is where you grew up?" she asked, taking in the huge stucco house, situated at the end of a cul-de-sac on an impressive span of acreage. "Nice digs."

"This is it." It took all Lucy's effort to contain the bundle of satin and lace in her grasp.

"The gates are locked," Nan said. "Are you sure you can get in?"

Lucy nodded. "Someone's always home."

Nan slammed the tailgate closed. "Okay, long as you're sure." She surprised Lucy by giving her a quick hug. "Sorry things didn't work out for you . . ."

Lucy shrugged. "Don't be. I think things are turning out for the best."

"Maybe. At least you got close—closer than I ever got. Well, I better be on my way." She waved before squeezing herself into the car, then waved again as she sped off.

Before the sound of the station wagon's engine had faded another car appeared, an aging yellow compact Lucy didn't recognize. She stared as it pulled up to the closed gates and stopped. Nervously she pressed the call button on the intercom by the gate, but nothing happened.

A young woman with short, dark hair sat behind the wheel of the yellow car. She cranked open her window and flashed a disarming smile. "Is this where the Walkers live?

Lucy nodded suspiciously, taking a few tentative steps toward the car for a closer look.

Recognition dawned in the driver's eyes. "You're Lucy Walker. Hi, I'm Andrea McClinton with the *Brennerton Times*."

*Egads, a reporter!* Panicked at the very idea of publicity, Lucy backpedaled a couple of steps and pressed the call button again. Still no one answered.

Andrea cut the engine and stepped out of the car with a reporter's notebook and pen in hand. "You're the person I wanted to talk to, anyway," she said, sounding friendly as a puppy. "Funny, you don't *look* ill."

"Ill?" Lucy said, her nerves transforming her voice into a squeak. Then she remembered the story her father said he'd given last night. "Oh, right." Instinctively she did not trust this woman with her too-nice smile. She pushed frantically at the button. Where *was* everyone?

"It's not morning sickness, is it?"

Lucy gasped. "No!"

"Then you're not ill?"

"Would you . . . would you go away, please? My father is the only one around here who talks to reporters." She was relieved to have remembered her stock defense against the press, drilled into her head by her father years ago.

"He wasn't too eager to talk last night. All he said was that you were sick and the wedding had been postponed." Andrea cocked her head to one side. "Care to comment?"

"N-no," Lucy said, looking at her feet. Dammit, she was stuttering.

"But you are planning to marry Arthur Sprague at a later date, right?" Andrea poised her pen on the page, as if to write down a quote.

The assumption made Lucy just angry enough to respond. "No, the wedding has been canceled. That's all you need to know." She jabbed again at the button.

"The whole town is speculating as to how and why you managed to disappear from your wedding," Andrea said, ignoring Lucy's dismissal. "How did you do it?"

Lucy answered with stony silence.

"You had help, of course."

"I didn't *say* that!" Lucy insisted, a bit too defensively, then wished she hadn't opened her mouth at all. She had just given herself away.

"Then you *did* have an accomplice? A lover, perhaps?" Andrea persisted, arching her dark eyebrows.

"Oh, for heaven's sake, he was nothing of the kind! I barely even knew him—" Lucy clamped her mouth shut and wished she could cut her own tongue out. She'd already admitted much more than she ever intended to. This sneaky little reporter, this youngster barely out of her teens, was turning her into mincemeat.

Andrea flashed a smug smile just as a voice came over the intercom. "Yes, who's there?"

Relief flooded through Lucy's whole body. "It's Lucy, Mother. Where have you been? Please, open the gates."

"Lucy, thank heavens," said Gwen as the electronically triggered gates crept open. "We were all out at the pool so we didn't hear you ringing."

By the time Lucy had summoned her courage to again order Andrea off the premises, the reporter was already climbing into her car. "Don't worry, I'm leaving. You've given me plenty to work with. Ha, and my editor said I wouldn't get a word out of you." The yellow car revved up and buzzed away, leaving Lucy to cough in its exhaust.

The trek up the driveway was a long one, giving Lucy plenty of time to dread the imminent confrontation. By now her family's anxiety had probably built up a good head of steam. She knew she was right when, the moment she walked through the front door and into the marbled foyer, they fell on her like ducks on a June bug. The four of them— her parents as well as Judy and Sandy—all tried to hug her at the same time.

She had to squirm out of the spiderlike embrace. "Goodness, you act as if I'm returning from the dead."

"We've been so worried," Gwen said, dabbing at her eyes with the edge of a handkerchief. "People have been calling—all last night, all this morning."

"We didn't know what to tell them," Sandy interjected. "How did you do it? How did you leave the church without anyone seeing you?"

"It was like you dematerialized," Judy added, her eyes full of curiosity and even a bit of grudging respect. Judy, with her offbeat sense of humor, was probably the only one in the family who would appreciate Lucy's acrobatic escape out the church window.

"Good Lord, that can't be your... is it?" Gwen paled slightly as she contemplated the bundle of white Lucy clutched.

Lucy nodded as she delivered the wad of crumpled satin and lace into her mother's outstretched arms. She wanted to apologize for the condition of the dress—it was, after all, frightfully expensive, and she hadn't intended to ruin it. But with all of them peering at her, she couldn't get the words out. If she could just talk to them one on one...

At last she focused on her father, who had said nothing. Though he was the least vocal, he was probably the most upset by her precipitous behavior. "I'm really sorry about the wedding, Dad," she said. "I just couldn't go through with it. I have a very good reason, but I can't... I can't talk about it."

Leon's forehead wrinkled with concern. "Lucy, sweetheart, you've always been able to talk to me. Maybe I can fix whatever's wrong."

It was true—she usually could talk to her father. They'd often engaged in spirited political discussions, and sometimes they had even talked about more personal things. But she simply couldn't bring herself to discuss Arthur's infidelity. "Not even you can fix it, Dad," she said with a wan smile.

"Art is absolutely desolate," said Sandy. "Whatever it is, can't you work it out with him?"

"Yes," Gwen agreed with a glimmer of hope in her eyes. "You at least owe him a face-to-face explanation. What you did . . ."

Lucy felt a slight twinge of conscience over her own cowardice. She knew she'd made the right decision where Art was concerned, but her behavior was hardly admirable. "I know it seems cold, running out on the wedding . . . oh, all right, I'll talk to him. But trust me, I don't owe Arthur a thing."

Four days later, Lucy had done what she thought was a competent job of putting her non-marriage to Arthur behind her. She'd talked to him, just as she had promised. She'd apologized for running out instead of facing her decision head on, but she'd made it very clear that the decision was irreversible. He hadn't taken it very well.

The following day she'd made still more apologies, to out-of-town wedding guests and anyone else who had been inconvenienced by the canceled ceremony. And she'd returned most of the gifts, much to her acute embarrassment.

With those responsibilities out of the way, she'd scoured the classifieds to find herself a new place to live. She'd sighed over a real estate ad featuring the gingerbread house in the hills Travis had mentioned, but had quickly moved on to more realistic prospects.

At last she'd settled for a small Cape Cod cottage in an older suburban neighborhood. It had a mammoth pecan tree in front and a fenced yard in back, and the owner had been willing to let her move in immediately. She was looking forward to getting away from her family, too. Though she loved them dearly, they were smothering her with their exaggerated concern over her emotional state.

On moving day she discovered just how difficult and manipulative Arthur Sprague could be.

He refused to let the moving company she'd hired have access to her belongings, all of which were locked inside his country house. He held hostage not only her clothes and furniture, but her computer, all her diskettes and a whole box full of work in progress. If she didn't get it all back, and soon, she'd lose weeks worth of work, miss all her upcoming deadlines, and ruin her reputation with her clients. He knew that, too.

Lucy paced her new and very empty kitchen, trying to progress far enough past her anger that she could come up with some plan of action. Why was Art doing this to her? She didn't delude herself into believing he carried some grand torch for her. More likely, he was simply committed to carrying out his threat. He had warned her, after all, that she would be sorry she hadn't married him.

Obviously the man wanted to play hardball, so she'd better not fool around anymore. She opened the yellow pages and looked under *Attorneys*. She could call Martin Hargrove, the Walker family attorney, but he always checked things out with her father before taking any action, and she would just as soon not involve the family any further. No, Lucy needed a lawyer who wasn't under her father's thumb.

*Townley, Miller and Blakeman*. The name jumped out at her, and a wave of pleasure washed over her at the thought of Travis Blakeman. He'd made the front page of this morning's paper with his announcement that he was running for mayor.

Travis would help her out, she thought, dialing the number. Then she stopped and hung up. She couldn't risk anyone linking herself and Travis together, not so soon after the wedding fiasco. That nosy reporter might still be snooping around. Lucy had been watching the papers, dreading the appearance of some nasty little story with Andrea McClinton's byline, but nothing had been printed.

She picked up the phone and dialed the number. She'd ask Travis for a referral. Surely that couldn't cause any problems for him.

Travis, sitting at his desk in the middle of drafting a complicated contract, was annoyed with the interruption and annoyed further that the caller wouldn't give her name. Not one of his regular clients, then. Still, he couldn't afford to be rude to anyone, even if he had no intention of taking on any new cases just now. He picked up the phone. "Travis Blakeman," he said, carefully modulating the irritation out of his voice.

"Hello, Travis, this is—"

"Lucy!" His annoyance immediately evaporated. He thought he'd never hear from her again, and he couldn't hide his elation at discovering her voice on the other end of the line. "Lucy, I was just thinking about you a while ago. In fact, I mailed a letter to your father just this morning. How are you doing?"

"Pretty good in general, thank you," she replied. "But I have a small problem, a legal problem and, well, you're the only lawyer I know."

So, this was a professional call, not a personal one. "I see. Why don't you talk to my secretary and make an appointment? I have some time free on Friday—"

"Oh, really, Travis, I don't think so. I just wanted a referral from you."

"A referral?" That puzzled him. Why wouldn't she trust him to handle the matter himself? "Tell you what. Why don't we have lunch. You can tell me about the problem, and then I'll know who to recommend." He glanced at his calendar and winced. His schedule was packed today. But he wanted to see her, if only to see for himself that she was getting along all right.

She hesitated. "I'd love to, of course, but I'm not sure you want to be seen with me."

Now he was truly intrigued. He was tempted to ask her to elaborate, but he was already running late for his next appointment. "How about Alma's Café, on Becker Boulevard? That's out of the way. In fact, most of my yuppie friends wouldn't be caught dead at a place like that, but I can't resist Alma's catfish. One o'clock?" He knew he was pushing, but something inside him refused to let her slip away again. He'd regretted walking away from her a hundred times since last Saturday.

"Well, okay. I guess that would be safe."

Safe? He couldn't wait to hear her explanation.

When Travis entered the bustling café a few hours later, he spotted Lucy immediately, though she was seated in a booth at the very back. He slipped past the hostess and headed toward the beacon of Lucy's brightly flowered dress and shiny red hair, which was pulled back from her face with tortoiseshell combs.

She greeted him with a smile that almost made his handshake go limp. "Thanks for seeing me," she said. "I know you must be busy."

"No problem," Travis replied easily as he set his briefcase on the seat across from her, then slid in after it. She'd never know how much effort it had taken to rearrange his appointments to squeeze in this lunch date, but he wouldn't have missed it for anything. If Lucy had a legal problem, he had a hunch it would be a doozy.

"Are you sure no one followed you here?" She looked anxiously out the café's plate glass windows.

"Like who? Lucy, please tell me what all this cloak-and-dagger stuff is about. If you were aiming for inconspicuous, you didn't dress the part."

She looked down at the brightly flowered sundress and blushed. "I didn't have much choice, which is part of the problem. But I'll explain that later. First I have to tell you—" She leaned forward and lowered her voice. "There's a reporter from the *Times* who seems determined to learn the truth behind why I canceled the wedding. She accosted me last Sunday morning outside my parents' house and, quite frankly, she tricked me into admitting more than I meant to."

A nibble of apprehension worked its way up Travis's spine. "What did you tell her?"

"I didn't mention any names, so there's no real cause for alarm. Just the same, she might be clever enough to put two and two together if she connects you with me. I didn't want to take a chance."

Lucy's concern for his reputation warmed him. Just the same, sneaking around wasn't his style. He'd made the decision to interrupt Lucy's wedding, and if it turned out to be a foolish action he simply would have to suffer the consequences. "If the story gets out, I'll deal with it," he said with more confidence than he felt. "If you ever get cornered like that again, just tell the truth. I don't want anyone lying on my account. The absolute truth is my best defense. It might be embarrassing, but I didn't do anything wrong."

She nodded. "Just the same, you watch out for that Andrea McClinton. I have a feeling she can twist right and wrong around her little finger."

Travis grimaced at the mention of Andrea's name. "I know about her. She's a real pain, fresh out of journalism school and eager to break her first big investigative story. I've already been warned to stay as far away from her as possible."

The waitress came to take their order. Travis already knew what he wanted—the catfish special—

but he waited for Lucy to make her choice. She took her time, finally settling on a hamburger and a chocolate malt, which she ordered in a voice barely above a whisper.

When the waitress had gone, he gazed at Lucy and considered how he wanted to phrase his next question. He had been curious about her shyness ever since she'd first mentioned it. "Does being shy cause a lot of problems for you?" he finally asked.

She shrugged. "I have my good days and my bad."

"But you're not shy with everyone, right? I mean, you've never been the least bit tongue-tied around me."

"Some people I can talk to—my family, close friends . . . and you. Most I can't, at least until I get to know them. My real problem, though, is when I'm the center of attention. That's when I lose it."

"But how do you cope?" he ventured. "Do you have a job?"

"Self-employed," she replied. "I'm a free-lance copy editor. Mostly I do academic stuff—textbooks, professional journals. My favorite is the *Arachnid Journal*, fondly know as *Spider Monthly*."

Travis grimaced. "A magazine devoted to spiders?"

"Yup."

"You make a living at this?"

She nodded. "It's the kind of thing I can do in solitude, and I like it that way. I have more work than I can handle. Which brings me to the main reason I wanted to talk to you. The aforementioned work is at this moment boxed up and stored at Arthur's country house, along with my computer, my furniture, my clothes and all my other earthly possessions."

"You mean Arthur refuses to return your things?" Travis asked, appalled.

She looked at her flowered dress. "He has just about everything except what I packed for the honeymoon. Fortunately I hadn't put my suitcase in his car yet, or he might have gotten that, too."

"Does he have a reason for behaving like such an ass?"

Lucy nodded. "Incredible as it may sound, he still thinks I'll change my mind and marry him."

What a pompous jerk, Travis thought, shaking his head as the waitress whisked their plates onto the table with a loud clatter. Lucy had a doozy of a dilemma, all right—not a terribly complicated matter, but a potentially explosive one. He was not at all sure Arthur Sprague was fully hinged.

"I do have some legal recourse, don't I?" Lucy asked.

"Yes, I'd say so. The problem requires filing a few papers and convincing a judge to order Arthur to relinquish your possessions. Shouldn't be difficult." He opened his briefcase and withdrew a stack of business cards bound with a rubber band. After thumbing through them for a few moments, he found the one he wanted. "Ah, here we go. Ed Price. He's young but very sharp. He won't waste your time." He handed the card to Lucy.

She flashed an unsteady smile and took the card, studying it briefly. "Thanks. I hope he's . . ." Her voice trailed off.

It took a moment for Travis to understand why she was apprehensive. When he did, he felt like an idiot. Ed Price would be a stranger to her. And she had trouble talking to strangers.

He whisked the card out of her hands. "Never mind. I'll get it straightened out for you," he promised. "Why don't you give me the details and I'll talk to Ed? Would you be comfortable with that?"

"I shouldn't put you to so much trouble. I'm being ridiculous." Just the same, she looked relieved.

"It's no trouble." He pulled a yellow legal pad and a silver pen from his briefcase and set them on the table. Between bites of the golden-fried catfish and hush puppies he jotted down the pertinent facts of the case. He made sure to get her new phone number.

By the time their plates were empty and two pages of the legal pad full, their business was finished. Travis glanced at his watch, knew he needed to get to the office and yet couldn't quite bring himself to terminate the meeting. His eyes kept straying to Lucy's lips and the way they puckered when she drew the last of the chocolate shake through her straw.

"Did you see the morning paper?" he asked.

"Yes, I did, as a matter of fact." She smiled expectantly. "The price of corn is down. Oh, and Buckley Hardware is having a great end-of-summer sale."

"You mean you didn't see—" He cut himself off as he realized she was teasing him. Soon his smile matched hers.

"Yes, I saw your picture three columns wide on page one. Congratulations. Did you say you'd contacted my father?"

"I put a letter in the mail this morning, which I'll follow up with a phone call."

She nodded her approval. "Would you like a friendly word of advice?"

"Sure. I'll take all the advice I can get."

"Strike now. Dad is all shook up about this annexation thing. He really wants it to pass. He owns some land just outside of town. It's ripe for development, but it's not part of any incorporated town. If the property gets annexed, he can get city utility service, and the land values will skyrocket."

"I'm in favor of the annexation," Travis assured her. He had his own personal reasons for wanting certain lands within city limits, but it would be good for the town as well, in terms of an increased tax base.

"Then you're aware of Wendall Cox's views regarding annexation."

"At the moment he's dead set against it. Thinks the city shouldn't grow, because that would lead to increased expenses for road maintenance, et cetera. Of course, that doesn't mean he won't take the opposite viewpoint if it'll give him more votes."

"Exactly. That's why you need to hit Dad up for support now, while he's still mad at Wendall. If our esteemed mayor suddenly changes his mind, he and Dad will be pals again."

Travis nodded. "I see. I'll call him first thing Monday morning."

"How do you feel about me running interference?" she asked tentatively. "I could talk to him, see how the wind's blowing, so to speak. I thought I might even arrange a meeting between the two of you."

He held up his hand in protest. "No, Lucy, I wouldn't want you to get involved. I wouldn't dream of imposing on our...your friendship." Friendship? Was that the right word?

"Why not? I'm imposing on yours by coming to you with my silly legal problem. Besides, you're not imposing. I happen to think you'd make a great mayor."

"Won't your father wonder how you know me?" Travis asked.

She waved away his concern. "It's enough for him to know I've read about you in the paper."

Something about her airy assertion twinged his conscience. She was advocating the telling of—not a lie, exactly, but a half-truth.

"Travis, there's not a political candidate in the world who wouldn't use a connection when it's offered," she added when he seemed reluctant. "You're too damned ethical for your own good, you know."

"There's no such thing as too ethical."

"Well, there's nothing unethical about what I've proposed. The whole thing will be extremely aboveboard."

She was quiet while he chewed on that idea for a minute or two. Her proposal was sounding more sensible by the minute. Not only would he get an inside track to Leon Walker, but he might have an occasion to see Lucy again—an important consideration, he thought with some surprise.

Her green eyes slid away from him for a few moments before returning, full of apprehension. "If you'd really rather I stay uninvolved . . ."

"No, you're right. I can't afford to turn my back on a legitimate connection. So, yes, by all means, talk to your father."

She gave him a tremulous smile. "I'll try to arrange a dinner for next week some time. Then you can come to the house, and we can be formally introduced in front of witnesses. That should prevent any unwanted speculation about our . . . friendship." She blushed.

It didn't take much to embarrass her, Travis realized. She still retained a trace of her shyness, even around him.

"If anyone should see us together," she continued, "they won't connect it to my botched wedding if we have a more legitimate reason to know one another."

"Will we be seen together?" he asked, deliberately putting her on the spot. But this was what the whole lunch had been leading up to, he realized.

She took on the look of a cornered fox. "I . . . I didn't mean to imply. . ."

"Well, I do. I've been trying to figure out just how we can see more of each other."

"You have a campaign to run," she hedged. "Maybe after—"

"Maybe after the election you won't be available. Anyway, I'm allowed an evening or two to relax during the campaign."

"It's not a good idea."

"Why not?"

In answer she pulled a twenty-dollar bill from her purse and dropped it onto the table. "That should cover lunch," she said, hastily scooting out of the booth. "I'll talk to Dad. Let me know what happens with the Arthur problem." She ran from the restaurant, with several pairs of eyes following her flight. For someone who doesn't like to be the center of attention, Lucy certainly could put herself in the spotlight.

Ah, hell, she was probably right. Now was not the time to launch a romance. His campaign demanded a hundred and ten percent of his time and energy. Just the same, he knew as surely as he knew the exact dollar amount in his campaign fund: he and Lucy Walker had some unfinished business.

# *Chapter Four*

Lucy appraised herself critically in the mirror and tried to ignore the butterflies in her stomach. It was only a small family gathering. She wouldn't encounter anyone she didn't know. There was no reason for her to be nervous.

All she had to do was survive an introduction to Travis Blakeman, pretending not to know him. Once she cleared that hurdle, no one would expect her to do more than murmur a polite word now and then. Still, she wondered if this was a bad idea after all.

It had been almost sinfully easy, getting her father to agree to meet Travis over cocktails at the Walker home. Leon hadn't thought the suggestion at all unusual, given that Lucy, unlike her sisters, had always taken an active interest in politics. She hadn't counted on her mother expanding on the invitation to include dinner, however, although perhaps Lucy should have expected it—Gwen did love to entertain.

Nevertheless, it was hard to say whether Lucy's little plan would bear fruit. Leon Walker didn't grant his support easily. But since Travis, as he was portrayed by the media, seemed to have all the right answers this early in the mayoral race, there was a good chance her father could be persuaded to back him—especially since Wendall Cox had not reversed his ridiculous stand on annexation.

So there was nothing to worry about, right? If only her darn hair would behave.

She formed her hairstyle for the third time, fluffing and shaping it into an elegant twist that was somewhere between the grandeur of her wedding-day ringlets and the simplicity of the straight style she usually wore. All the while, she kept chanting to herself that there was nothing to worry about.

She added one final spritz of cologne. If there was nothing to worry about, why did the butterflies in her stomach feel more like pterodactyls, with teeth and sharp claws?

She was finally forced to admit that her attack of nerves had nothing to do with the size of the gathering, or whether Travis would gain the support he sought. It had everything to do with the prospect of seeing Travis again.

He'd been so easy to talk to; that was before she'd discovered he was interested in her—interested in *her,* Lucy Walker. Suddenly she was concerned about what she'd say, how she'd look, what he'd think of her. And for the first time she was nervous about facing him.

She'd blow it. She knew she would. That was probably for the best, since she couldn't see how she and Travis were at all suited. Once he discovered what a quiet, dull life she led, he would agree with her, and that would be that.

Taking small comfort from that conclusion, she examined the back of her hair one last time, checked her stockings for any stray snags she might have missed, then forced herself to turn off the bathroom light and be on her way.

The driveway gates were open when she approached the house. A quick survey of the cars present told her Travis wasn't here yet. Good. She was in no mood to make a grand entrance for him. She parked around back, so her ancient Volkswagen bug wouldn't offend anyone's sensibilities.

She found her father with Sandy and Don, Sandy's husband, in the library, enjoying a bottle of white wine—a dusty one, apparently from Leon's private cache in the cellar.

"Lucy, my word, *look* at you!" Sandy shrieked the moment she caught sight of her sister.

Lucy glanced down at herself, certain some part of her anatomy was hanging out of her tiny black dress. The salesgirl who'd sold it to her had assured her that it was just the cut to make the most of her petite stature and hourglass figure, but now Lucy wasn't so sure. She wasn't accustomed to revealing in public even a small amount of cleavage, or any part of her leg above her knee, unless she was at the beach.

"What's wrong with the way I look?" she finally asked when she could find nothing amiss in her appearance.

"It's just that you look so...elegant! Sophisticated."

"You can say that again," added Don with a tad too much enthusiasm, earning a withering stare from his wife.

Leon merely smiled indulgently as he poured her a glass of wine. She accepted it with a smile, took a tentative sip, then inclined her head appreciatively. "Mmm, good stuff."

"You always did have a discriminating palate," Leon commented with a nod of approval. "Your sister here has been whining because I won't make her a strawberry daiquiri."

"I can't help it if I don't like wine that tastes like an old piece of wood." Sandy set her half-empty glass on the mantel. "C'mon, Don, let's go find Judy and Charlie. They'll want to see this." She nodded meaningfully toward Lucy before exiting, husband in tow.

Lucy sighed. "It's not as if she's never seen me dressed up before. Heavens, how many of these little dinners have I endured over the years?" she asked her father with a careless shrug.

"Don't mind her. You do look pretty tonight, sweetheart. How are things going? Have you talked to Arthur?" he asked, sounding anxious but trying not to.

"More than I ever care to," Lucy answered through gritted teeth. Just the mention of the man's name filled her with a murderous rage. "But in answer to your first question, things are going fine." She didn't intend to mention that Arthur was still holding her belongings hostage. Thanks to Travis's help, however, her unsuspecting ex-fiancé would be served with a tidy set of legal papers in the morning, ordering him to relinquish her possessions immediately.

The doorbell made her jump.

"Ah, that's probably our guest now," Leon said, rising from his chair. Then the phone at his elbow rang, and he reflexively reached to pick it up.

Lucy started for the door herself, paused indecisively, then continued when her father urged her with a gesture of his hand. Answering the door at her parents' house was something she seldom did—she never knew whom she might encounter. But her mother was probably up to her elbows in phyllo dough, and Lord only knew where her sisters were. She couldn't leave poor Travis standing on the porch.

She trekked across the marbled foyer, steeling herself for the bit of theatrics to come. She opened the massive front door with a jerk, then felt her breath whoosh out of her at the sight of Travis Blakeman standing on the front porch in a sedate gray suit.

"Hello," she managed, fixing her eyes on the lovely bouquet of tiny pink roses he held in one hand.

"Hello, yourself. Hey, look at me," he demanded gently. "You look beautiful, Lucy."

She looked at him then, putting a finger to her lips. "We're not supposed to know each other, remember?" she whispered as she let him inside. Then, in a slightly louder voice she said, "The flowers are beautiful."

"They're for your mother," he said, then whispered, "but I'd rather give them to you."

He was flirting with her! Even as she felt a blush creeping up her neck, she gave him a look that warned him to watch his step.

That was the last moment she had Travis to herself for a long while. The family immediately descended on him. Leon, cordial but still a tad standoffish, took his role as host very seriously and introduced everyone to their guest. He saved Lucy for last.

"And the one who answered the door—that's Lucy, my middle daughter. She suggested we get together, as a matter of fact."

"I'm pleased to meet you, Lucy," Travis said, shaking her hand then giving it an extra, conspiratorial squeeze.

"My pleasure," she replied, amazed at how well she was carrying this off.

"So, you're already following the mayoral campaign?" he asked her politely.

"I read the paper," she said with a coquettish tilt of her head. This wasn't so bad, she decided. Why had she been so terrified earlier?

Gwen put a solicitous arm around her daughter's shoulders. "She reads several newspapers from cover to cover every day," she elaborated. "She's always had a keen interest in politics."

"I saw you on TV the other day, Mr. Blakeman," Judy piped up.

Travis's attention shifted smoothly to Lucy's younger sister. "Did you? Call me Travis, please."

"Why don't we all move into the library," Gwen suggested. "I understand Leon has unearthed some exceptional wine from the cellar."

"Oh, you collect wine?" Travis asked with just the correct amount of sincere interest. "So does my father."

He was good, Lucy mused. And yet she had a feeling that Travis's friendly attitude wasn't the slightest bit calculated.

"Your father—William T. Blakeman, right?" Leon asked as they all filed into the artfully decorated library, which smelled pleasantly of leather and furniture polish. "Helluva businessman, so I've heard."

The conversation moved in polite areas for the next several minutes. Lucy settled into a chair, letting her second glass of wine warm and relax her. Her family, sensitive to her usual shyness, would never have deliberately drawn her into the conversation, but Travis did, asking her several pointed questions that required more than a yes or no answer. Amazingly, she handled it fine. She even managed to tell one brief anecdote about one of her father's campaigns, and everyone laughed.

Gwen glanced at her watch. "Oh, my, I have to look in on dinner. Lucy, dear, would you help?"

"Sure, Mother," Lucy answered with more enthusiasm than she felt. She hated to leave the scene when she was doing so well.

The huge, ultra-modern kitchen was filled with the scent of seafood pastry. With practised efficiency, Gwen removed the elegant dish from the oven and set it on a cooling rack, then stirred a large, glass bowl filled with glazed carrots before popping it into the microwave. Last, she removed a tureen of vichyssoise from the refrigerator and examined its consistency.

"Everything looks wonderful, Mother," Lucy said. "What do you need me to do?"

"Nothing, really," Gwen confessed. "But I did want to have a word with you. What do you think of Travis Blakeman?"

Lucy shrugged. "He's young, but I think he'd make a very good mayor."

"And on a personal level?"

Again, she shrugged. "I hardly know him." Somehow she managed to sound noncommittal. She picked up a sponge and busied herself with wiping down the already immaculate countertop.

"You can't fool me, you know," Gwen said quietly. "I've seen the way you look at him. I could always tell when one of my girls had a crush—"

"A *crush?*" Lucy interrupted, horrified. "Mother, I'm twenty-five years old. I'd like to think I'm a little beyond getting infatuated over every good-looking male who happens to cross my path."

"Then you do think he's good-looking?"

"Of course. I'd have to be blind not to notice that. But I'm not infatuated, and don't you go getting that matchmaking look in your eye." She

couldn't bear the thought of anyone pushing Travi
toward her. If anything were to develop betwee
them, she wanted to see it happen naturally.

"I had no intention of matchmaking," Gwe
said haughtily. "Actually, I'm quite relieved to hea
you say you're not interested."

Lucy hadn't said precisely that she wasn't inter
ested, but she would let that slide. "Why?"

"It's so soon after Arthur... You need som
time, I think, to decide what you really want—"

"It was Art who didn't know what he wanted,'
Lucy grumbled. Or maybe he did. He wanted to b
married to the state senator's daughter and have hi
little cupcake on the side. Still, her mother wa
probably right. Love on the rebound was a ba
idea.

"Anyway, Travis Blakeman certainly isn't you
type," Gwen finished offhandedly. "Mmm, the vi
chyssoise turned out well this time. Would you tak
it into the dining room, please?"

"Sure." Lucy reached for the ornate silver tu
reen, then stopped. "What do you mean, he's no
my type?" she asked, struggling to maintain th
same offhand tone as her mother.

"Isn't it obvious? He's a politician. How man
times have you said you don't care for the breed
despite your father's career?"

That was entirely true, Lucy mused uncomfort
ably.

Gwen put a companionable arm around her daughter's shoulders and squeezed. "I just can't imagine you as a politician's wife. What with public appearances, cameras, constant entertaining— you'd be miserable. No, you need another type of man altogether—the strong, quiet type. A nice accountant who'll take care of you. And you'll find him someday. It will just take a very special man to see all your special qualities." She kissed Lucy on the cheek before releasing her. "We'd better get dinner on the table before poor Mr. Blakeman faints from hunger."

Lucy wiped at the lipstick she knew would be on her cheek. Her mother's careless comments had struck home. A politician's wife—what a horrible thought. She could never do all the things her mother had done over the years.

Not that there was any reason to fear such a fate where she and Travis were concerned. After all, a light flirtation wasn't a marriage proposal. Still, the observation had put a damper on Lucy's ebullient mood.

She found herself seated across the massive dining room table from Travis during dinner. As always, Gwen's meal was a huge success, but Lucy hardly tasted it. She found herself staring surreptitiously at Travis as he parried her father's pointed questions with ease, simultaneously catering to Judy's often vacuous observations and pretending not to notice Sandy's haughtiness. In between, he managed to say just the right things about each course.

He was good, Lucy thought again, not to mention incredibly sexy. And way out of her league.

"What do you think about it, Lucy?" Travis asked.

Everyone stared at her. She was mortified to realize she hadn't been following the conversation.

"I agree with Dad," she finally said. That was about the safest response.

Travis nodded pleasantly and turned his attention to Leon, who now waxed eloquent about toxic waste, which apparently was the issue Lucy had lost track of. At the same time, Lucy felt something touch her leg. With a start she realized it was Travis's foot, minus its shoe. As he deftly kept up his end of the conversation, he ran his toe up and down her sensitive calf, sending delicious shivers coursing through every part of her body.

What nerve! she thought even as she struggled not to smile. To try to woo money from Leon Walker was brave enough, but to make improper overtures toward his daughter at the same time was downright reckless. Travis did not strike her as a reckless sort. What was he thinking of?

"Who's ready for dessert?" Gwen asked brightly at the first break in conversation.

"I'll get it," Lucy volunteered, darting from her chair. Travis gave her a covert smile before she escaped to the kitchen.

Lucy survived dessert by carefully shifting her legs out of his reach.

After dinner, it was Leon's antiquated habit to retire to the library with the other gentlemen for cigars and brandy. Usually no one smoked cigars but Leon, and he seldom got takers for the brandy, but he maintained the custom anyway. The only reason the Walker women had never objected to their exclusion was because they suspected the event was boring as all get out.

Anyway, the Walker females had their own custom—picking apart their male dinner guests. Poor Travis was no exception.

"He's enough to make a girl swoon," observed Judy as she helped clear the table. "I can't believe he's not married. He'll get the women's vote, that's for sure."

"He's too young and too cute," Sandy said. "How could he possibly be a competent mayor? I'm voting for Wendall."

Lucy made a hissing sound.

"Well, Wendall always sends us the nicest Christmas presents."

"That's an excellent reason to cast a vote in his favor," Lucy commented, her sarcasm evident.

"Well, so what did you think of him?" Sandy pushed. "He was obviously hanging on your every word—" She stopped when their mother gave her a warning look, which didn't escape Lucy's notice.

Truth was, she didn't know what to think of Travis. Nothing in her life had prepared her for the tumultuous feelings just hearing his name provoked. "It's stuffy in here," she said, abruptly setting a pile of dishes in the sink and heading for the French doors. "I'm going outside for some air."

She escaped to the solitude of the patio. It was hardly refreshing, since the air was hot, humid and still. But at least she was alone with her thoughts.

She settled into a plastic patio chair and stared out over the glowing, sapphire-blue swimming pool, wishing she knew what to do.

Travis was making a pass at her, no doubt about that. Part of her thrilled at the chance to explore the potential there. He seemed to bring out a part of her she usually kept hidden—the clever, articulate part. But now she knew she couldn't give in to the attraction. She was capable of falling hard and fast for Travis Blakeman, a situation that could never work in the long run. Her mother, however innocently, had pointed that out with great clarity.

She sighed her disappointment aloud, and silently wondered how long she could stay out here. She didn't want to face Travis again, but she supposed it would be rude not to say goodbye.

Inside, Travis listened with half an ear as his host expounded on his own campaign experiences. This room was the last place he wished to be right now, not when that luscious little redhead was mere footsteps away.

Lord, she looked like a million bucks tonight, he mused. But no wonder she was shy. Her family hovered around her as if she were an invalid, anticipating her every word and saying it for her before she got the chance. Didn't they see how clever and insightful she was? The two sisters were personable and vivacious, true, but Travis didn't see any reason Lucy should allow them to overshadow her as she did.

The conversation turned to sports, something the two brothers-in-law could relate to. Travis commented when appropriate and wondered how soon he could make a gracious exit without jeopardizing his chances of winning Leon's support.

He almost shouted with relief when the older man suggested they rejoin the ladies, then almost wilted with disappointment when he discovered that Lucy wasn't among the bevy of redheads drinking coffee in the living room.

He waited a few minutes, accepting a cup of decaf from Mrs. Walker, but when Lucy didn't appear he had to ask where she was. "I need to be leaving soon," he explained, "and I wanted to thank her again for suggesting we get together."

Gwen looked around, seemingly surprised that one of her brood was missing. How could anyone not miss her? Travis wondered.

"She's still on the patio, Mom," Judy said.

"Oh, that's right." Gwen set down her cup. "I'll go and get her."

"Don't bother," Travis said quickly, seizing what appeared to be a golden opportunity. "I'll just step out and tell her goodbye." Before anyone could suggest otherwise, he set his coffee down and made a beeline for the French doors he'd glimpsed off the kitchen.

He opened the door quietly, immediately spotting Lucy. She sat in a patio chair with her back to him, facing the swimming pool. The pool's blue lights cast an intriguing halo around her fiery hair.

She didn't hear him approach. He tiptoed up behind her, leaned over and placed a warm kiss on the nape of her neck.

Lucy gasped and shot out of her chair, then seemed to sag with relief when she realized who had assaulted her. "Travis Blakeman, what do you think you're doing?"

"Exactly what it felt like. Kissing the back of your neck. I've wanted to kiss you all night long." He stepped around the chair, trying to move closer to her, but she deftly sidestepped him, keeping the chair between them.

"This isn't a good idea," she said. "Not here, not now. Won't you be missed?"

"I told your folks I was coming out here to tell you good-night, which is what I'm trying to do if you'd stop skittering away from me."

She looked at her watch. "I didn't realize it was so late," she said overbrightly. "I'm sure you need to get home." She moved as if to head inside, but Travis stepped in her path and deftly pushed the chair aside.

"Lucy, why are you so nervous all of a sudden? You've never been nervous around me before."

"You never tried to make a pass at me in front of my whole family before."

"Your family's not here now," he pointed out, reaching toward her and gently grasping her bare upper arms. Her skin felt incredibly soft and alive under his touch. "Just tell me no, and I'll leave without a whimper."

"This is not a good idea," she repeated. Her voice shook, though she didn't resist when he drew her into the shelter of his arms.

"Was that a no?" he said when he'd wrapped her securely in his embrace.

"I guess not," she whispered just before his mouth closed firmly over hers.

If he'd expected a shy, tentative kiss from her, he was delightedly disappointed. Lucy Walker kissed as if she thought she could put out the fire that had flared between them. Her efforts were instead fueling and fanning the flames. Her lips came sweetly alive under his, open and warmly accepting even as she trembled against his chest.

Travis's swift, sure response startled him. After only a few moments of pure heaven, he pulled away, breathing heavily of the hot, humid air, and wondered how he could have been so sure of himself only a few heartbeats ago. He'd thought he was some kind of smooth character. What a total idiot.

"What's wrong?" she whispered.

It was a moment longer before he could manage the words. "Nothing, it's just that . . . you're a bit of a surprise. And I think maybe you were right when you said this wasn't a good idea."

"No?" she asked, looking a bit dazed herself.

"Not that I didn't enjoy it, but...another time." It took an amazing amount of strength on his part, but somehow he extricated himself from the embrace and set her firmly away from him. "Good night, Lucy."

She watched him stride purposefully away. It wasn't until he'd disappeared inside the house that her wits began to return. He had pulled a jumble of raw emotions out of her with that kiss—dragged them right out into the open, for anyone who was looking to see.

Just as she'd predicted only minutes ago, she was falling fast and hard for Travis. She'd had no idea how quickly her prediction might come true, but at least it wasn't too late. Not yet.

One by one she collected her tangled feelings and, without examining them too closely, locked them away where they belonged.

*Another time,* he'd said. She wished now she'd had the presence of mind to tell him there would be no other time. The thought made her feel empty and sad inside.

## Chapter Five

It was a rare, cool summer morning. Lucy sat on her back porch sipping black coffee and taking advantage of the northern breeze. Arthur had grudgingly relinquished the last of her possessions two days ago, and now she was playing catch-up with her work. She hadn't missed any deadlines yet, but the pile of manuscript pages she had to plow through during the next week was daunting.

The phone rang; she could hear it through the screen door. Normally she paid it little attention. She'd learned not to allow anything to interrupt her work, always letting the answering machine handle the phone. But for the past five days, ever since the dinner at her parents' house, she'd kept her ear cocked whenever the phone rang.

It was Travis again. The voice made her breathing come a little faster. She hopped up from her lounger, manuscript pages flying every which way, and rushed inside to listen to the resonant tones pouring out of the answering machine.

This was the fifth time he'd called in as many days, and the fifth time she hadn't responded.

"Lucy, if you're there I'd really appreciate it if you would pick up the phone . . ."

She poised her hand above the receiver, plagued by indecision. Oh, Lord, how she wanted to talk to him. But she had to make Travis understand that she wasn't available. Short of telling him so, which she couldn't bring herself to do, ignoring him sent the clearest message.

"All right . . . this is the last time I'll call." He hung up decisively.

Lucy flinched at the finality of the noise, then gave a hopeless sigh. She'd done it this time. He was out of her life for good now. Idly she rewound the message tape and listened again. Even in anger, his voice made her heart swell inside her chest and brought her close to tears.

No man had ever affected her this way—certainly not Arthur. Why did Travis have to be involved in politics? And why did her mother have to be so confoundedly correct? Travis wasn't the man for her. Or, more accurately, she wasn't the woman for him. He just hadn't realized that yet.

Determinedly, she erased the message, and all the others that she'd saved on the tape. It was over. Finished. Kaput. And she had work to do.

She returned to the patio and picked up the manuscript pages that had scattered in the breeze, then spent the next five minutes putting them in order and finding her place. The subject of brown recluse spiders held little interest for her at the moment, but she forced herself to concentrate on the highly technical article.

Before long her red pen was flying, all thoughts of Travis banished to the nether corners of her mind.

"So you are home."

Lucy jumped, and the pen flew out of her hand. Of course, she knew who would be standing there before she even looked up. But the sight of him stole her breath away. He was devastatingly handsome in light beige summer trousers, starched white shirt with the sleeves rolled up, navy blue tie and blue suspenders. Even the frighteningly stern scowl on his face didn't mar his good looks.

"Hi, Travis." Her voice squeaked as she tried to sink farther into the lounger's plastic-covered cushions. All she could think about was how awful she looked in her baggy gym shorts and T-shirt.

He scooted her legs to one side of the lounge chair and sat down on the edge. "You're not answering your phone," he said calmly.

"I . . . I don't answer my phone while I'm working," she hedged, indicating the pile of papers in her lap.

"You haven't called me back, either. Your answering machine message states very clearly that you'll return the call as soon as possible."

"I, um, I've been so busy . . ."

"Okay, Lucy, let's cut the baloney. You're playing games with me and I don't like it. You should know right now that I can't take a hint. If you don't want to see me, you'll have to say so right to my face."

She tried to find the words to do just that, but of course she couldn't, not when he was searching her face with those gorgeous whiskey-brown eyes, and the only words that wanted to spring to her lips were, *Yes, yes, yes, I want to see you.*

He softened in the face of her silence. "I'm coming on a little strong, aren't I?" he questioned almost sheepishly.

"You could say that," she agreed.

"I probably shouldn't have kissed you like I did the other night."

"It did seem reckless, especially for you. I had you pegged as a cautious type."

"I am," he was quick to say. "Normally I am, anyway. But something about you brings out my impulsive side. I can't explain it. All I know is I don't want to let it go without a fight."

His sincerity touched her as nothing else could. "There are a million and one reasons we shouldn't see each other," she argued sensibly.

"Name one."

She thought for a moment. "What you just said. I make you act impulsively, something you definitely don't need when you're trying to get elected mayor."

"I'll control myself. Try again."

"There's still the possibility of that dreadful Andrea creature linking you to my botched-up wedding," she reminded him.

He dismissed that concern with a wave of his hand. "It's been two weeks. If anything were going to come of that, the story would be printed by now. Name another."

"You're in the middle of launching a political campaign. Trust me, you won't have time for a social life."

"Even a candidate is allowed an evening off every once in a while. It'll keep me sane. Invalid reason. Name another," he challenged.

"Are you going to make me elaborate on all million and one?"

He nodded. "Possibly."

"Okay." She took a deep breath. "We aren't right for each other."

"How do you know?" he shot back. "We haven't even been out on a date."

"But we're so different—"

"In some ways, not so different in others."

She slumped back in the lounger, defeated for the moment. She couldn't tell him the real reason she was afraid to see him—that she'd lose her heart and *then* have him realize it couldn't possibly work.

"You're not missing Arthur, are you?" he asked.

She made a face. "Don't make me retch."

"Then go out with me. I have two tickets to see *Camelot* at the Starlight this Friday."

Without meaning to, she sighed. She loved *Camelot,* and she loved the open-air Starlight Theater in Kansas City.

"Is that a yes?" he asked. The boyishly hopeful note in his voice did her in.

"Yes," she finally agreed. "At least in Kansas City we won't be recognized."

"Now why are you concerned about that? There's not a thing in the world wrong with me dating the daughter of one of my biggest supporters."

It took a moment for that to sink in. "Dad?" she asked. "You mean he came through?"

Travis nodded smugly. "He confirmed this morning. He's even planning to host a small fundraising dinner in my honor."

"That's marvelous!"

"So you see? Everything's turning out okay."

She wasn't so sure about *everything*, but she wisely kept mum. She'd already accepted his invitation; she'd have to go through with it. She would just keep the evening light, she concluded. Maybe after the one date Travis would see what a mismatch they were and give it up.

He liked her little bungalow, Travis decided as he approached Lucy's front door early Friday evening. It was painted a bright blue with white shutters—cute and compact, just like its occupant.

As he rang the doorbell, he cautioned himself not to be so pushy. He had never been the type to aggressively pursue a woman—in fact, he couldn't remember a time he'd ever done so, even in high school. He simply didn't bother with women who weren't readily available. Why would he waste his time, he'd always thought, when invariably another desirable female waited just around the corner?

Nor had he ever wasted much time or energy thinking about any specific woman, or wishing he could be with her.

Lucy was changing all that.

His timing was lousy; she'd been right about that. The election was only three months away, and almost his every moment until November was spoken for. Helluva time to be in hot pursuit of a woman he couldn't get off his brain for more than five or six consecutive minutes.

Still, he didn't intend to give up, though he had every intention of lightening up. No more footsies under the dinner table with her father looking on, and definitely no more soul-stirring kisses in the moonlight. He'd take this slow and easy. He would date her—just take her for an occasional evening out, nothing more. Maybe he'd be able to cure himself of her and still find time to win the election.

He knew he was fooling himself the moment she opened the door. She was an emerald-green vision in a shimmering silk shirtdress exactly the color of her eyes.

"You're early," she said with a half smile.

That was another first. He'd never been early for a date. "Want me to go away and come back?"

"Don't be ridiculous," she said, letting him into the house. "I just need a few minutes to do something with my hair—"

"Leave it down," he said abruptly.

"Pardon?"

"Leave it down—please," he added. "It looks pretty." Like a curtain of red fire, he wanted to say, so bright he thought he might burn himself if he touched it. He shoved his hands into the pockets of his khaki dress slacks. Then he had a look around the living room, to distract himself.

Empty boxes and piles of crumpled newspaper attested to the fact that she was still settling in, but even so Travis got a pretty good feel for what the room would look like when she was done unpacking. The pale blues, greens and pinks in her furnishings were coolly soothing; the puffy furniture, inviting. It was the sort of room a person could spend a lot of time in.

"You got your things back from Art, I see," he commented.

"Not without a struggle," she said from where she stood in front of the hall mirror, brushing her hair. "Art was most ungentlemanly about it."

"But then you already knew he wasn't a gentleman."

"If I haven't thanked you for helping me out—"

"It was no trouble." He had enjoyed it, actually, enjoyed serving papers to that contemptible worm. In the end he'd decided not to involve Ed Price, the other attorney. It was such a small matter, after all.

"I assume I'll be getting a bill," Lucy said.

"I hadn't planned on billing you, no. It took so little time—"

"Then I'll have to make a campaign contribution, won't I?" she asked, turning toward him with a mischievous sparkle in her eyes. She slung the strap of a tiny leather purse over her shoulder and they were off.

"Lucy, why do you keep glancing over at the side mirror?" Travis asked fifteen minutes later, when he sensed she wasn't listening to a thing he said.

"What? Oh, it's probably nothing . . ."

"What kind of nothing?" he pressed.

"A yellow car behind us. It looks just like the one Andrea McClinton drives."

The very thought gave Travis a sick feeling in the pit of his stomach. "Well, so what if it is?" he asked, forcing a carefree tone to his voice. "We're not doing anything disreputable by enjoying an evening at a perfectly respectable theater."

"I wouldn't underestimate her," Lucy said ominously, peering over her shoulder. "Her kind can cause more trouble than a cat at a dog show. When she confronted me she was determined to find out what went wrong with my wedding."

"As long as our behavior is circumspect, I don't see any problems." Just the same, Travis increased the pressure on the accelerator. "Surely a reporter has better things to do," he added.

"I don't know. A few years back, there was a reporter in Jefferson City that just about drove Dad crazy. The man was convinced Dad was a walking graft machine and set out to prove it. Dad finally had to press harassment charges to get the guy to stop.''

''I'm sure we're worrying for nothing,'' said Travis. ''Look, the car just took that last exit.''

''It did?'' Lucy swung around and squinted out the back window. ''Well, thank goodness. Guess I'm just being paranoid. But I'd hate it if my silly wedding-day stunt got you in trouble.''

''It was as much my doing as yours,'' he reminded her. ''Don't give it another thought.''

She relaxed after that, keeping up her end of an animated conversation for the next hour. Travis was relieved that she showed no signs of the shyness she'd exhibited at her parents' house. He liked the idea that he was special to her in that respect—that he was one of the few people in the world with whom she could relax and be herself.

He soon found they had more in common than an interest in politics. They both loved vintage science fiction movies, Mickey Spillane novels and Southern cuisine—the greasier the better. Why did she think they were wrong for each other? he wondered. He'd have to ask her about that, but not tonight. He wouldn't take any chance on spoiling the mood.

As it turned out, a surprise thunderstorm did a rather thorough job of spoiling if not the mood, then their carefully laid plans. They had no more than found their seats at the intimate outdoor theater when a threatening bank of thunderclouds rolled in from nowhere and cut loose, drenching them thoroughly before they had a chance to find shelter. In the midst of a crowd of disappointed and uncomfortable theatergoers, they could do nothing but laugh at their misfortune.

Lucy turned her face up to the rain and shook herself like a wet kitten. "This is what we get for living in the Midwest," she said good-naturedly when they finally reached an overhang that offered a bit of protection.

Travis laughed in agreement as the rain trickled uncomfortably down his neck. He looked at himself, at the shirt plastered to his skin, then at Lucy. He could honestly say she looked even more attractive wet than dry. Her thin silk dress clung unmercifully to her rounded breasts and hips, giving her a raw, elemental look—as if she'd just sprung from the sea.

The evocative imagery sent his pulse racing. He wanted to be alone with her, to peel the wet silk off her body and taste the rain on her skin. At the same time, he knew what he wanted was impossible. To become seriously involved with her wouldn't be fair to either of them, not with the precarious state his life was in at the moment.

The rain showed no signs of letting up, so the performance was canceled. Only vaguely disappointed, Travis held Lucy's hand as they meandered to his car, unmindful of the rain.

"I'm sorry about your dress," he finally said as he unlocked her car door. "It's ruined, isn't it?"

"Not at all. It's washable silk. In fact, it'll dry in no time."

Feeling only slightly less guilty for forgetting an umbrella, he climbed into the driver's seat and started the engine. Traffic kept them stuck in the parking lot for awhile, so he turned on the heater to chase off the unexpected chill. "Would you like to do something else? Dinner, maybe?"

"Will anyone let us in looking like drowned rats?" she countered. But Travis knew of a casual jazz club in Waldo where patrons paid more attention to the music than each other, so no one would give two slightly damp visitors a second look.

Once there, he couldn't convince Lucy to dance—she claimed to have two left feet—but they shared a plate of fried mozzarella at a dark corner table, and then held hands as they fell under the spell of the singer's dulcet tones.

It was still fairly early as they made their way home, and Travis was not anxious to end the evening. Impulsively, he took the turnoff that led to Taluka Lake. He could vividly recall how the water had danced with moonlight the last time he was here, and how enchanting Lucy had looked beside it. He'd regretted not taking her in his arms that night, and now he intended to make up for it. He dismissed his earlier vow to avoid any and all moonlight kisses. Some chances simply were meant to be taken.

"Isn't this the way to the Hide-Away Lodge?" Lucy asked.

"Uh-huh."

"How is your sister, anyway?"

"Oh, same as always, I guess. I talked to her yesterday. She's going to organize the distribution of my campaign posters."

"That's quite a job."

"I tried to warn her, but Nan has a big heart. She'd do anything for me."

Lucy nodded in agreement. "She was awfully nice to take me in the way she did. I'm not sure if I even thanked her properly." She glanced at the illuminated dial on her watch. "Isn't it a little late for a social call?"

Travis hadn't planned to bother Nan, but apparently Lucy thought a cozy visit was his intention, and he didn't know how to break the news to her that what he really wanted was to ravish her. Oh, well, it wouldn't hurt to pop in and at least say hi. "Nan is a night owl," he said. "She never goes to bed before two or three. Anyway, I'm sure she'll get a kick from seeing the two of us together."

All the lights were on in the motel's main building. When Travis parked the car and then went inside, they found Nan playing hostess to a whole flock of night owls, drinking coffee and playing cards in the dining room.

"Well, look who the cat dragged in!" Nan boomed as soon as she saw the visitors. She hoisted herself out of her chair. "Velma, honey, play my hand for me, I have to go kiss the future mayor of Brennerton." Her comment elicited the attention of everyone in the room.

Travis felt Lucy stiffen beside him, her eyes wide with what could only be described as terror. Instinctively she grabbed for his arm and secured it in a death grip.

He should have anticipated this, Travis thought as Nan descended on them, her blond hair wilder than ever. Because Lucy was generally open and relaxed with him, he tended to forget about her shyness. Gently he extracted his arm from her talons and returned his sister's hug. "Nan, you remember Lucy Walker, don't you?"

"Why, of course! How are you, darlin'?" She enveloped her in a hug every bit as warm as the one she'd given Travis. Then she turned and addressed the room in general. "Don't worry, folks, he's just my brother. And this is the one I was telling you about, the bride who—"

"Nan!" Travis interrupted, taking a firm grip on his sister's arm. "Think you could get us some coffee? On second thought, why don't we *all* go get some coffee in the kitchen?''

Nan took the hint. "Oh, right. Deal me out a few hands, would you?'' she called to the card players before leading the way through the swinging door in the back of the dining room. Travis had to nudge Lucy out of her fear-induced paralysis before she would follow them into the large, functional kitchen.

"I know, I know, I wasn't supposed to tell anyone about that,'' Nan said as she busied herself with the controls on the industrial-size coffee maker. "There's nothing to worry about. All those folks are from out of state. They never heard of Brennerton, or Travis Blakeman, or Leon or Lucy Walker. No harm done.''

Seeing Lucy's white face, Travis wasn't so sure. "You just embarrassed the hell out of Lucy, you know,'' he said curtly as he slipped a protective arm around Lucy's shoulders. Even as he said that, he realized he was doing exactly as Lucy's family did—protecting her, coddling her. How could she possibly get past her shyness if everyone encouraged her to pull into her shell whenever the going got tough?

Nan whirled around to face them with a stricken expression. "Oh, Lucy, I forgot. You don't like to be fussed over, do you? I'm so sorry.''

"It's all right, really,'' Lucy said, at last finding her voice. "Being shy is my problem, not yours.''

Then she turned to Travis. "You didn't have to bite her head off," she scolded.

Travis raised his eyebrows, but said nothing.

"How 'bout some fresh strawberry pie to go with the coffee?" Nan asked brightly, apparently unaffected by Travis's chewing out.

Travis, as usual, couldn't resist anything from his sister's oven. His irritation dissolved. He and Nan chatted as he demolished a generous slice of the pie, but Lucy, though she listened to the conversation with seeming interest, said little and was obviously uncomfortable. Travis kept his eye on her, hoping she'd relax, but when she didn't he drained his coffee quickly and suggested they be on their way.

"Sorry about that," he said as they stepped outside into the warm, humid breeze.

"About what?" Lucy asked.

"Putting you through that when all I really wanted—"

"You didn't do anything wrong. I'm the one who embarrassed you."

"Embarrassed me?" He put his hand at her waist as they negotiated the steps down the porch, then deftly guided her onto the path that led to the lake instead of toward the car.

"By acting like a tongue-tied ninny."

"I wasn't embarrassed. A little concerned, maybe... all right, the scene was awkward all the way around. That's not your fault."

They walked onto the pier and stood exactly where they'd stood the first night they had come here. The moon was new rather than full this night, but the effect was no less intoxicating.

"Travis . . ." she began uncertainly.

"What is it?" He touched her hair, an impulse he'd been resisting all evening.

She reached up and gently stilled his hand. "It *is* my fault. All social scenes are awkward when I'm around."

He smiled indulgently. "It can't be as bad as all that."

"It *is*," she insisted, so emphatically that Travis's smile faded. "I want you to understand that. You're a very social person. You have to be. I'm not."

It was a sobering realization. Travis took a step away from her so he could think more clearly. "Are you saying I couldn't take you to parties and introduce you to my friends?"

"You could, but I'd be about as exciting as a cantaloupe."

"I couldn't bring you to my parent's house for dinner?"

"Again, you *could* . . . I'd do it if you really wanted me to. I've suffered through hundreds of awkward dinners, and one more wouldn't kill me. But I can almost guarantee you it wouldn't turn out well."

It couldn't be that bad, he thought. She had to be exaggerating. "Maybe it's something we can work on," he suggested, running his fingers along the smooth line of her jaw.

She ducked away from his touch. "Travis, pay attention. I've been this way all my life. I won't change. I wish I could, but I can't."

"Then I guess I'll just have to keep you all to myself." He caressed her again. She didn't duck away this time, but her eyes were big and sad, and he hated it that he couldn't make her smile.

"I just don't want you to have false expectations," she said.

"The only thing I'm expecting right now is a kiss. Think you can handle that?" She allowed him to pull her to his chest. He cradled her head against his shoulder and stroked her hair, wanting to protect her from the world and seduce her all at the same time.

How could his arms feel so good around her, Lucy wondered, when she knew it was all wrong? The longer he held her, however, the more right it felt. She'd been as honest with him as she knew how. She'd given him the brutal truth, and he hadn't thrown up his hands and walked away. Maybe she was looking for trouble where none existed. If he wasn't worried about her shyness, maybe she should worry a little less.

That thought filled her so full of hope, she turned her face upward, intending to give him that kiss he'd asked for. But the look of pure, unadulterated hunger in his eyes made her suddenly aware of his hard body against hers, the solid planes of muscle under her hands, the subtle scent of his after-shave, and she knew a mere kiss would never be enough. His sheer maleness made her feel feminine and desirable in a way that was foreign to her.

"Lucy," he whispered as his mouth descended on hers.

It was not a gentle kiss, yet she reveled in the firm, commanding pressure of his lips. He plundered her mouth with his tongue as if to claim her as his territory, and his hands tangled themselves in her hair.

Even when his hands wandered lower, to massage her breast through the thin silk of her dress with a soft yet insistent pressure, it seemed as if that, too, were his privilege. His bold touch felt somehow right, as if such intimate contact were somehow preordained, and she had no desire to stop him.

When he shifted his attention to her ear, teasing it with the tip of his tongue, she felt her knees wobble. She laced her fingers through his thick, curly hair and held on for support. When he traced a path of a dozen kisses along her neck to the hollow of her throat, she forgot to breathe for a few seconds.

No mere physical sensations had ever enthralled her so completely. She could only whimper when he unbuttoned the top of her dress and tasted the skin that peeked out from her lace bra.

He stopped suddenly, breathing like a marathon runner as he laid his cheek against hers. "I want to see all of you, Lucy. I want to make love to you like I've never wanted anything in my life."

"Here?" she squeaked as her hormones skidded to a halt and her common sense returned.

"Here, your house, my house, on the moon—I don't care where."

She shook her head even as she took hold of his hands and gently pulled them away from her body. "No. Much as it pains me to remind you, you're the one who suggested we be circumspect in our behavior. This is definitely not circumspect."

He laughed, despite his distress. "Oh, God, I forgot. I can just see the headlines: Mayoral Candidate Tumbles Senator's Daughter on Public Beach."

Lucy didn't think that was funny. "You'd better not forget," she said, buttoning her dress. But she softened the reprimand with a quick kiss to his cheek. "Just remember, from now until November, your behavior has to be beyond reproach. I refuse to put your campaign at risk any more than I already have."

He laughed again and brushed his lips against her rain-softened hair. "You're something else, you know that? An inferno one minute, all fussy and practical the next."

"You can see I'm right, though, can't you?"

"Unfortunately, yes. Lucy, just tell me one thing," he said as they made their way up the path hand in hand, the fire between them banked but not quenched, not by a long shot. "If I weren't running for mayor, would you..." He didn't finish the question, deciding it was futile.

"In a heartbeat," she answered softly.

# Chapter Six

Travis's intercom beeped, followed by the strident voice of his secretary, Lisa, interrupting his dictation. "Mr. Blakeman, there's a reporter from the *Brennerton Times* here to see you."

He switched off his recorder and picked up the phone. "Does he have an appointment?"

"It's a she. And no," Lisa replied. "No appointment, but she's quite insistent."

Travis glanced at his calendar; he had twenty minutes free before his next client was due. He sighed. "All right, send her in." Glad-handing the press was already getting to be a chore, and the mayoral race hadn't even begun to heat up yet. But so far he'd come off smelling like a rose, despite the

*Time*'s decidedly yellow bent. He forced a smile and hoped it would pass as sincere.

His smile froze when Lisa opened the door and escorted into his office a young, dark-haired woman who brought an aura of disaster with her. The reporter approached his desk with her hand outstretched, smiling much too smugly. "How do you do, Mr. Blakeman? I don't believe we've had the pleasure. Andrea McClinton."

Travis gave her hand a perfunctory shake, his mouth pressed into a grim line as he fought an overwhelming sense of impending doom. This was bad. Definitely bad.

"Would you like coffee?" Lisa asked as she headed out the door.

"No, thank you," Travis answered, not giving Andrea a chance to reply. "Now, then," he said when the door had closed, "what can I do for you? I have only a few minutes—"

"Should be plenty of time," Andrea interrupted, sitting briskly in one of the maroon leather chairs opposite his desk. She pulled a reporter's notebook out of her purse and flipped it open. "I'll get right to the point. Did you, or did you not, spirit Lucy Walker away from her wedding?"

Though her question appalled him, Travis hid his horror behind a placid expression. "What does this have to do with the mayoral race?"

"Not a thing," Andrea replied confidently. "I'm working on a story for the life-style section on Ms. Walker's wedding, or lack thereof. I've been trying to get to the bottom of that little mystery for quite some time, now, and I think I've figured it out."

"Have you?" Travis raised one skeptical eyebrow and leaned back in his chair, as if amused by the exchange.

Andrea pushed a pair of half glasses onto her nose and looked at her notebook. "Fact. On the afternoon of the Walker-Sprague wedding, the church parking attendant saw a dark blue Fiat stop in a no-parking zone, and a man fitting your description run inside the church.

"Fact. Minutes later, said man drove away in said Fiat. Fact. Lucy Walker was subsequently found missing. Later she admitted that someone, a man, had helped her flee from the church."

Not enough, Travis thought triumphantly. The woman was fishing. "Interesting," he commented.

"My contact at Motor Vehicles informs me yours is the only dark blue Fiat in town," she said.

"People from all over the state attended that wedding," he countered. "Kansas City probably sports dozens of blue Fiats."

Andrea gave an exaggerated sigh. "Fact. Your name appears as counsel of record on a court order directing Arthur Sprague to relinquish Lucy Walker's belongings."

*Damn.* He should have let Ed Price handle that little matter after all. "So? I'm Ms. Walker's attorney. Anything else?"

Her expression indicated she'd saved the best for last. "Fact. You and Lucy were seen driving out of town together on July the twenty-seventh. Later that same night you were seen entering the parking lot of a motel near Taluka Lake."

So, Andrea McClinton *had* been tailing them. Barely containing his urge to lunge across his desk and throttle the brat, he steeled himself for the rest. Just how close had she gotten? Had she witnessed their empassioned embrace at the water's edge? Had she crept up and listened to the heated words he'd spoken to her?

"Do you deny any of this?" Andrea asked when he failed to respond.

"I don't deny or confirm, Ms. McClinton. I have no comment, as you are delving into my personal life where you have no business. Furthermore, I'd like to offer you a word to the wise. You're treading on very dangerous ground. If you print a story that even hints at an untruth, I'll press charges."

Andrea cocked her head and studied him for a long moment. "You're a public figure, Mr. Blakeman. To make a libel charge stick, you'd have to prove malice."

"I may be a public figure, Ms. McClinton, but Lucy Walker isn't." He was gratified to see a brief expression of uncertainty cross Andrea's face, so he pressed his advantage. "Furthermore, to print a word of what you're insinuating constitutes reckless disregard for the truth, in my book."

She sat up straighter. "Nonsense. I'm trying to verify the story. I'm giving you every opportunity to correct me if I'm wrong."

She had a point, dammit. He folded his arms and stared out the window, searching desperately for some way out of this dilemma. Maybe Lucy had been right when she'd said he was too honest, but he could not bring himself to lie, not even to the likes of Andrea McClinton. But neither could he bear the thought of Lucy's reputation being maligned when he could prevent it.

"Well?" Andrea prompted.

He decided he had to clear up one matter. "My sister owns the motel you mentioned," he finally said. "Lucy and I paid her a visit on the night in question. We sat in the kitchen and drank coffee for approximately twenty minutes. We took a short walk by the water, and then I took Lucy home."

Andrea scribbled furiously. "And what about the wedding?"

"That's all the time I have, Ms. McClinton," he said, standing.

She stared at him defiantly for several seconds, as if contemplating whether to push her luck. At last she looked away and gathered her things. "It's been most interesting, Mr. Blakeman.'' She stood, gave him a regal nod and turned on her heel.

Travis expelled a long breath when the door closed behind her. Would she print the story? he wondered. Maybe, maybe not. She put on a brave front, but when it came right down to it, not many reporters would risk a libel suit, especially when such questionable motives and methods were employed. The *Times*'s editor was partial to a racy brand of journalism, true, but he wasn't an unreasonable man. He knew where to draw the line.

Fortified by that bit of reasoning, Travis picked up the phone, grateful for an excuse to finally call Lucy. They'd agreed not to see each other for awhile, so that things could cool off, and Travis had been regretting that decision ever since. Campaign or no campaign, circumspect or not, he wasn't sure how much longer he could stay away from her—especially since he'd gotten a taste of the passionate nature she kept so well disguised.

Halfway through dialing, he changed his mind and hung up. If he told her about Andrea, he'd only worry her, probably needlessly. Andrea McClinton was full of hot air—he'd bet on it.

Truth was, he had another matter he wanted to discuss with Lucy, and he didn't want to do it over the phone—or worse, put up with that blasted answering machine of hers. Instead, this evening he would drop by unannounced. It seemed the best way to catch her and pin her down, which was what he intended to do.

Lucy leaned over to place a heavy glass dish in the oven. She enjoyed cooking; trying out a new recipe was usually a sure cure for the doldrums. Today, however, she just couldn't get excited about chicken enchilada casserole. For the past week she'd been alternating between a racy adrenaline high and a snake-belly depression, and all because of Travis Blakeman.

Just thinking about the way he had kissed her, and the way she'd responded, sent her pulse skittering into an uneven rhythm and put a spring in her step. But then her spirits would plunge when she remembered how she'd insisted he not see her again, at least not until he'd had a chance to think about his priorities. And of all the unreasonable men— he'd listened to her! It had been almost a week since their date, and he hadn't called.

The doorbell rang as she was setting the oven timer. ''Come in, Judy,'' she called out. Her younger sister had said she'd drop by with a housewarming gift that evening.

She heard the door open slowly. ''It's not Judy,'' a deep voice called. ''Can I still come in?''

''Travis?'' Her heart beat wildly as she made her way to the front door, noticing as she passed the hall mirror that she looked a fright. Too late to do anything about that now. She grabbed the door and opened it the rest of the way. "What are you doing here?"

He leaned against the door frame, looking the epitome of confident masculinity in faded jeans and a casual cotton shirt. "Paying a social call."

She looked down at her cut-offs and neon-green T-shirt, deciding at that moment she had to do something about her wardrobe. She let him in, thankful that at least the house was in reasonably good order.

"You don't seem too pleased," he ventured as she led him into the living room.

She smiled then. "It's not that. I'm just surprised. I thought maybe..." She sank into one of her modern, cushy chairs, finding the words difficult.

"Maybe what?" he prompted.

"That maybe you'd decided to do the smart thing and stay away from me."

"I couldn't," he said simply, giving her a look hot enough to defrost her freezer. "You said I needed to think about my priorities, and you were right. That's just what I've been doing." He sat on the sofa across from her, his warm brown eyes never wavering. "The campaign is important to me. I owe it to my supporters to put a hundred and ten percent of my time and effort into winning it."

She looked at her feet. "I see."

"But that doesn't mean I have to completely trash the rest of my life. Now, you and I have started something, and I don't intend to drop it."

Her heart filled her chest like an inflating balloon. Still, she forced herself to be practical. "But how will we—"

"I'm getting to that. Obviously I can't add more hours to a day. So the solution, Lucy, lies with you."

"Me?"

He nodded. "On your goodwill, your kind understanding, your endless patience."

She raised one skeptical eyebrow. "Why does this sound like a campaign speech?"

"I'm serious, Lucy. My schedule is guaranteed to be a mess and I'm apt to be distracted for the next few weeks. Can you tolerate seeing me at a moment's notice? Or that I might be exhausted when we can find time together? Or that our dates might get interrupted or canceled altogether sometimes? I know, it sounds like a terrible situation, but the alternative is worse."

"What alternative?"

He leaned forward, resting his elbows on his knees. "Not seeing each other at all. Frankly, I don't consider that an option."

Her heart swelled again. "I can be flexible," she said with a deceptively casual smile.

His eyes sparkled with a light all their own as he grinned at her. "After the election, I swear I'll make it up to you. I'll spoil you rotten with all the attention I'll give you."

"Is that another campaign promise?"

He shook his head. "It's more substantial than that. Come here," he said, reaching out for her.

She hesitated. It was the physical nearness that had gotten them into trouble at Taluka Lake. Their only salvation had been their public location, which had instilled in them some measure of caution. Now, in the privacy of her home . . .

He stood and closed the distance between them, taking one of her hands between his. "Don't worry, I've got my head on straight this time. I'm not planning to rush anything. It wouldn't be fair to either of us, not when things are going to be so unsettled for awhile. I just want to hold you a minute, that's all."

She wasn't sure if she was relieved or disappointed, but she let him pull her to her feet and into his arms. He hugged her, and the feel of those strong arms folding protectively around her was enough to convince her she was disappointed. But he was right, darn it. It would be stupid to rush anything at this point.

"Mmm, what's in the oven?" he murmured into her hair.

The oven? Who could think about food at a time like this? "Chicken enchilada casserole," she answered when he released her a few moments later and she could think again. "Did you just invite yourself for dinner?"

"Yup."

She gave a fatalistic shrug. "I said I'd be flexible. Guess I'd better start now." She only hoped she could find two dishes that matched. Some of her kitchen boxes were still stacked in the garage.

Seated in the casual breakfast nook that overlooked the backyard, Travis was halfway through his second helping when he remembered the other reason he'd come tonight. "Your father set a date for the fund-raiser," he said. "Three weeks from this Friday. It'll be a sit-down dinner at the River Inn with a jazz band afterward, so get out your dancing shoes."

She toyed with her food and said nothing.

"Lucy?"

"You want me to go with you to th-that?" she said, mortified over the telltale stutter.

"Oh, I forgot—you don't dance, do you? I could give you lessons," he suggested hopefully.

His optimism brought a lump to her throat. "It's not that, Travis, it's just—"

"All right, you don't have to dance. You can eat, though." He nodded toward her plate. "I know you can eat."

"Not in front of a room full of people, I can't. Every eye in the place will be on you, and if I'm your escort they'll be watching me, too. I'm sorry, I just can't do it."

There was a long pause. "You're really serious?"

"Yes. I'm flexible, but I'm still a chicken at heart."

He sighed. "Okay, I have an alternative. You don't have to go as my date. We can both come stag, and rendezvous in the coatroom when no one's looking."

"Travis!" A giggle chased away the threat of tears. He was trying so hard.

"All right, forget that last part. Tempting, but too risky. But Lucy," he said, turning serious, "the dinner is important to me, and you're important to me. I'd like you to be there."

She looked up, amazed at the feeling behind his words. Was she really important to him? He dropped his gaze, as if a tad embarrassed at his admission. How could she say no to him when he looked so hopeful?

*No. N-O.* Crisply enunciated. She gathered her small reserve of determination around her. "I wish I could say yes, but believe me, I wouldn't win you any votes. If I tried to talk to anyone I'd stutter. I wouldn't be able to eat a bite of the food. And I definitely wouldn't dance."

"That doesn't matter," he insisted. "You'll look so gorgeous, no one will notice if you don't say much. They'll just think you're silent and mysterious." Even as he prompted her, he wondered if he was doing the wrong thing by pushing her. But he didn't want to coddle her the way her family did, either. He stuck to his guns.

Lucy took a deep breath. "No, I won't do it," she said again. "But I'll—I'll come with my parents. I'll be there for you, even if no one knows it but you and me."

The doorbell rang again, stalling any further argument. Travis decided he'd let her win this round. At least she'd conceded to come to the dinner, apparently in itself a difficult feat for her.

"Yoo-hoo, sis, are you home?"

Lucy shot Travis a wary look before answering. "In the kitchen, Jude." And then, in an undertone, "The cat's out of the bag now."

Judy breezed into the kitchen, her arms overflowing with a towering arrangement of blue and peach silk flowers and a chocolate sheet cake.

Travis sprang to his feet. "Here, let me take something." He relieved Judy of the flowers just as Lucy hopped up to save the cake from falling icing first onto the floor.

"Thanks," Judy said. "I was about to—" She stopped abruptly, staring first at Travis, then at Lucy.

"You remember Travis Blakeman, don't you, Judy?" Lucy said smoothly, secretly a little pleased that she could shock her unflappable younger sister.

"Oh, sure." Judy shook Travis's proffered hand, though she still appeared a trifle puzzled.

"Nice to see you again, Judy," he said with his usual friendly smile. Then he turned to Lucy. "Sorry to eat and run, but that's the story of my life these days." He pecked her on the cheek, a kiss that said everything and nothing. "I'll see myself out."

Judy stared at her sister with raised eyebrows and a gaping mouth until they heard the door slam. "You and Travis Blakeman?" she squeaked. "He did seem taken with you at dinner, but..." She gasped and put a hand to her mouth. "Does this have anything to do with why you and Art—"

"No!" Lucy snapped. "I met Travis *after* I decided not to marry Arthur." Actually, the two events had happened simultaneously, but why quibble over a few paltry seconds?

"Then you knew him before the dinner?"

Lucy sighed. "Yes. We didn't mention it because I didn't want to invite any unwarranted speculation, that's all."

Judy squealed. "I'm dying, he's so cute. Are you going out with him? Or did I hallucinate that kiss on the cheek?" She dragged Lucy to the breakfast nook and sat her down in one chair, then took the other one. "Tell me everything or face the consequences."

Finally, Lucy gave into the urge to divulge a sisterly confidence. "We've been out once. And he asked me to attend the fund-raising dinner with him."

Judy squealed again. "That's terrific! That's ... that's awful!" she said when she realized the implications. "All those people, and he'll be right in the spotlight. You can't do that, can you?"

Lucy shook her head. "I told him no, and now I'd like to kick myself."

"You're doing the right thing," Judy said positively. "Although I don't know how you did it. It would be awfully hard to turn down those big brown eyes—oops, don't tell Charlie I said that. The cake's for him, by the way, it's his birthday. I was hoping you'd help me decorate it. And the flowers are for you."

Lucy stood and walked to the counter to have a closer look at the silk blooms. "They're beautiful. They'll match my furniture perfectly. Thanks, Jude."

"You're welcome."

"And of course I'll help you decorate Charlie's cake. While we're doing that, maybe we can think of a way I can see Travis without destroying his political future."

By the time they had completed their elaborate decorating efforts, there appeared to be more red-icing flowers than cake, and still the two sisters hadn't come up with any solution to Lucy's dilemma. There didn't seem to *be* any answer, not even a workable compromise. A man like Travis Blakeman didn't belong with a socially disastrous woman like herself, Lucy concluded grimly.

She didn't want to accept that.

On a late August night three weeks later, Lucy stepped into an ice-blue taffeta evening dress and felt a surprising thrill of confidence. She knew she'd never looked more sophisticated. The price of the dress had squeezed her budget unmercifully, but she was determined to look her best for the fund-raising dinner.

The off-the-shoulder style was a 1950s throw-back that made her appear more slender and willowy than she would have thought possible. Vintage crystal jewelry and long white gloves enhanced the fifties image. She'd French braided her hair, inter-weaving strands of tiny blue beads with the red tresses.

She was carefully applying her lipstick with a shaking hand when the doorbell rang. Glancing at her watch as she hurried to the door, she realized she was running late and was glad of it. If she'd had to sit idly waiting for her parents to pick her up, she might have used the time to work up a good anxiety attack.

She opened the door and gasped. Travis stood on the porch appearing outwardly dashing and dignified in his tux, as a candidate should. But the smoldering look in his eyes was anything but dignified.

Lucy's face grew warm under his hungry gaze. "What are you doing here?"

"I thought I'd try one last time to convince the best-looking woman in the city to be my date tonight." He was holding two large, perfect camellias. He brushed the soft, fragrant petals of one against her cheek before handing the flowers to her.

"They're beautiful," she gasped, grateful for something to focus her attention on besides herself. "I'll just run and find a vase or something to put them in." Even as he reached for her she turned swiftly and headed for the kitchen. She had enough adrenaline in her system already without adding the extra excitement his nearness caused.

She was running water into an empty mayonnaise jar—the best vase she could come up with—when she felt warm, firm hands at her waist and the press of Travis's lips at the back of her neck. "Travis..."

"Won't you reconsider?" he asked tenderly.

She'd never been so flattered in her life. To have a man like Travis go to all this trouble... but he'd live to regret it if she capitulated now, and she'd hate herself. "I can't," she said even as she reveled in the feel of his warmth against her back. She had seen little of him since the night they'd shared the casserole in her kitchen. Not that she begrudged him—she knew the campaign had to come first. But she'd felt his absence as keenly as if they'd been longtime lovers.

"Mmm, then let's just skip the dinner," he said between nibbles on her ear.

"Good idea. You didn't want to be mayor anyway."

He placed a possessive hand against her hip and squeezed it impertinently before releasing her. "Spoilsport. Are you sure?"

She nodded, though at that moment she wasn't sure of anything.

He left without asking again.

Oh, what was wrong with her? she berated herself a few minutes later as she climbed into the back seat of her parents' Lincoln. This was Travis's night to shine and she'd started it out on a sour note. All he'd asked her to do was try. She thought of the frustration she'd seen etched into his handsome face, and she knew she would have traded a decade of her life not to have disappointed him.

She took a deep, calming breath. Next time, she thought. The next time he asked, she'd go, no matter what the occasion. She didn't want to think about the fact that there might not be a next time.

* * *

The River Inn was a gracious old hotel on the limestone bluffs overlooking the Missouri River, and the fanciest digs in Brennerton. Leon Walker had hosted many a party there, always receiving excellent food and faultless service. It was no wonder he'd chosen it for tonight's dinner.

The large banquet hall was lavishly decorated with silk flowers and garlands of ribbon featuring Travis's blue-and-gold campaign colors. The ceiling was swimming with blue and gold helium balloons. Lucy immediately recognized her mother's touch in the decorations. Gwen obviously had been having a field day doing what she did best.

The hall was already filling with Travis's supporters, who had paid fifty dollars a plate for the privilege of enjoying the bash. Lucy recognized many of the faces, though at that moment all names were a blank.

"Ah, here's our guest of honor." Leon, always instinctively attuned to who was present or absent in a room, located Travis immediately. Lucy, moving in her father's wake, was soon enveloped in a knot of tuxedoed men and silk-clad women, all vying to shake the candidate's hand. They of course paid her no attention, for which she was grateful. Even when Travis's gaze passed inevitably to her and he held out his hand in a casual greeting, no one seemed to think much of it.

"Nice to see you again," she murmured, forcing herself to breathe slowly and evenly. This wasn't so bad.

She experienced only a moment of irritation when he moved immediately on to shake hands with a tall, blond woman, who managed to extract him from the group and walk away with him. He was, after all, taking the limelight with him and away from Lucy, for which she ought to be grateful. If she'd wanted him at her side all night, she could have gone as his escort. Still, she stared at him until another group surrounded him and obscured him from view.

"So, my little girl has her eye on the future mayor," Leon said softly.

Lucy's head snapped around as she stared at her father. "Am I that obvious?"

"Judy told me. And you're here, which says a lot. You won't even come to *my* campaign parties."

"I might have made a mistake by coming," she acknowledged. "Although I've been here ten minutes already and nothing horrible has happened."

She felt a hand on her shoulder and turned, expecting to see her sisters or her mother. But her ready smile froze on her lips. She'd spoken too soon. Something horrible was standing beside her. Arthur Sprague, every one of his blond hairs neatly in place, kissed her on the cheek as if he had the right.

She reflexively wiped at her cheek with her hand. "What are *you* doing here?" she seethed.

He gave her a cocky grin. "I paid my fifty dollars like everyone else. I wanted to get a close-up look at the man who caught you on the rebound."

She shot a nervous look toward her father, hoping he might somehow rescue her from this awkward situation, but he had stepped away from her to talk to someone. "News travels fast," she muttered. "And I am *not* on the rebound."

"Should be an interesting evening," Art said, giving her one final, measuring look before sauntering away.

Lucy felt the hairs on the back of her neck stand on end. What was he talking about? If he did anything to spoil this night for Travis, she would break his kneecaps!

She ought to warn Travis, she decided, just in case. She cast about the room for him, relieved to spot him working his way toward her bearing two glasses of wine.

He offered one of them to her. "I thought you might want something. It's quite a crush at the bar."

"Thanks." She drank half the glass in one gulp. "Arthur is here."

"You're kidding. Where?" Travis looked around him with an angry scowl.

"Over there, talking to the woman in the purple dress. I don't know what he intends, or why Dad even allowed him in here, but he'll stir up trouble if you let him."

"Of all the nerve!" Travis growled. "I ought to toss him out on the sidewalk."

"No, no, you can't do that—not until he does something that warrants it. I just want you to be on your guard, that's all."

Travis took a deep breath and blew out slowly. "You're right," he said. "Arthur Sprague can't do anything but embarrass himself. We'll just forget he exists." He smiled suddenly, deepening his one irresistible dimple, and ran a finger along her hairline to her ear. A delicious chill ran all the way down to the soles of her feet.

"Arthur who?" she said.

Travis leaned over and whispered in her ear, "Rendezvous in the coatroom in ten minutes?"

She laughed nervously. "You have a whole room full of people to schmooze. You can work your charms on me another time."

"Is that a promise?"

She was prevented from answering by the noisy approach of her two sisters and their husbands. The men shook hands with Travis as Judy and Sandy shot Lucy a series of nervous glances. It soon became apparent that something was troubling them.

"We have to talk to you, Lucy," Judy said in a stage whisper. "Now."

Figuring Travis could work the room more easily without her, she allowed her sisters to escort her away.

"What's going on?" she demanded when they were out of anyone's earshot. "If this is about Arthur, I already saw him."

"It's worse, much worse," Sandy said ominously as she half-dragged Lucy into the ladies' room. As soon as they'd made sure they were alone, Judy opened her purse and pulled out a crumpled sheet of newspaper.

"It was delivered just before Charlie and I left the house," Judy said as she unfolded the paper and handed it to Lucy. "There, at the bottom of the page. Is it true?"

Lucy's eyes swam, but not enough, unfortunately, to blot out the headline.

*Walker Wedding Fiasco: Bride Jumped Out Church Window into Candidate's Arms.*

# Chapter Seven

"I think I'm going to be sick," Lucy said, sinking onto the padded bench in the ladies' room.

Sandy put her hands on her hips and glared. "You don't have time to be sick. We've got to *do* something or we're going to have a disaster on our hands. When Dad gets wind of this he's liable to take a swing at your precious candidate. I can't believe you put your own father in this awkward—"

"Oh, Sandy, put a sock in it," Lucy said wearily, pressing a hand to her head in a vain effort to stop it from spinning. "What does the damn story say, anyway?"

Judy read it aloud. By the time she was finished, Lucy's anger overrode her nausea. Arthur obviously had had something to do with the tone and timing of the article; he came off sounding like a candidate for sainthood. It appeared as if Travis, on the other hand, had deliberately plotted to ruin the wedding, seduce Leon Walker's innocent daughter and then use that connection to get to Leon.

"Is it true, Lucy?" Judy asked softly.

Lucy shook her head adamantly. "On the surface the statements are true, but a few key elements of the story are missing," she said. Then, as quickly and succinctly as possible, she told her sisters how and why Travis had come to the church that day. "When I found out what a complete jerk Arthur was, I should have simply called off the wedding, but...well, you know how difficult that would have been, making a big public announcement of the fact that I'd been made a fool. I just couldn't face it."

Her sisters nodded, no longer condemning. "You were already in quite a state," Sandy said.

"So there I was," Lucy continued, "and there was the window, and Travis just happened to be there, that's all. He didn't even know I was Leon Walker's daughter at the time, and it was all my idea to get Dad to support Travis. Travis doesn't have a conniving bone in his body."

"That's all fine and good," Sandy said, "but Dad's still going to explode like a Roman candle when he reads this. He'll be a laughingstock."

"Then I'd better go find him and show it to him right now," Lucy said, standing determinedly. "That way at least I can explain—" She cut herself off when the bathroom door opened.

Gwen entered, outwardly calm and controlled, as always. But the look emanating from the depths of her eyes could have crumbled a brick wall. Apparently Judy wasn't the only one to read the paper that evening.

"What happened?" Lucy asked, scarcely breathing the words.

Gwen managed to answer with dignity. "Well, the last I heard, your father was threatening to hang your boyfriend from the chandelier."

The evening went downhill from there. Leon was beyond reason by the time Lucy reached him. Her anxiety tied her tongue so thoroughly she was useless, and he was in no mood to listen to a word of explanation from Travis. Judy's and Sandy's attempts to smooth ruffled feathers merely convinced Leon that Travis had brainwashed his entire family.

To make matters worse, word of the disagreement was spreading like a flu virus throughout the banquet hall. As tempers flared, every eye in the place was covertly monitoring the escalating argument, and every ear strained to hear a stray word drop that would clue them in as to who was winning.

Only Gwen maintained her composure. "It's too late to call it off," she reminded her husband. "There are a hundred and seventy-five plates of chicken cordon bleu stacked in the kitchen ready to be served, and the band is already setting up in the ballroom. Let's just get through the evening as best we can and straighten it out tomorrow."

"Tomorrow we can sweep up the ashes," Leon corrected her. "You can stay if you want, dear, but I've seen quite enough." He turned to Travis. "Blakeman, you'd better enjoy yourself this evening, because this party represents the last penny you'll get from me or anyone in my camp. If you want to continue in politics, you'd better move to another state."

Lucy flinched at the harsh words. Her father was a formidable man when he was angered, like a baited lion, and she couldn't recall seeing him quite this outraged. He swept imperiously out of the room, speaking to no one. After a moment of indecision, Gwen followed.

Travis started to go after them, to try one last time to persuade Leon Walker to listen to the truth, but a reporter from the *Times* stepped in his path, attempting an interview. Travis's first impulse was to punch the intruder between his beady little eyes. It was his rag, after all, that had caused this uproar. But some self-preservational instinct prevented him from assaulting the guy, which would have led to more detrimental press coverage. Instead he calmly listened to the man's questions and answered each as best he could.

Inwardly he was floundering, trying to assimilate all that had just happened. He'd never in a millenium have guessed that one small, albeit impulsive act on his part—revealing to a bride that her fiancé was a cad—would have escalated into such a cataclysm.

He wasn't foolish enough to believe he could salvage anything from this mess. Leon Walker was a beloved, well-respected community leader in Brennerton. His condemnation spelled the end of Travis's campaign.

As for his budding relationship with Leon's daughter... Lucy. Oh, hell. In all the hubbub he'd forgotten about her.

"Sorry, but you'll have to excuse me," he said to the reporter even as he frantically scanned the room. But she'd vanished along with the rest of the Walker clan. He spent the next ten minutes searching for her, but she was gone.

His inclination was to leave, too. But running away was no solution. Here was a roomful of people who had paid fifty dollars a head for the privilege of supporting his bid for office, and he owed them some explanation. He started decisively toward the podium just as he heard his name being called. He stopped and turned to see Nan barreling toward him, a look of pure agony on her broad face.

"Oh, Travis, I've been looking everywhere for you," she said, breathing heavily. She stopped abruptly and closed her eyes, as if bracing herself for something unpleasant. "Hit me. I deserve it. Just hit me and get it over with. I'll feel better."

"Nan! What are you talking about? I've never hit you in my whole life."

She opened her eyes again. "It's all my fault," she said, her words barely above a whisper and her eyes brimming with tears. "I'm the one who spilled the beans to that reporter. Only I didn't know she was a reporter at the time, I swear, Travis. She said she was a tourist from out of state—"

"Shh! It's all right, Nan," he said, putting a brotherly arm around her shoulders. "She already had most of the story before she found you. It's not your fault. Are Mom and Dad here?" he said quickly, changing the subject. He was not equipped to deal with a hysterical sister just now.

"Yes," Nan replied, sniffing back her threatening tears. "They don't know quite what to make of the article. Dad said he at least wants to meet this woman you tossed away the campaign for."

He may never get the chance, Travis thought as he gave Nan's shoulders a parting squeeze. Lucy might not ever come out of her house again after this traumatic experience.

Again he headed toward the podium, stopping to exchange uneasy handshakes with several friends and acquaintances on his way. An air of expectancy came over the banquet hall as he approached the microphone. Some obviously knew what the controversy was about, while others could only guess that something odd was afoot. Everyone was anxious to hear Travis's speech.

Travis was more than a little anxious. He didn't know what he was going to say until the words came out of his mouth.

"Good evening," he said, amazed at how sure and steady his voice sounded. "Our host, state representative Leon Walker, was scheduled to introduce me this evening. Many of you already know why he chose to forgo that dubious honor."

A titter of nervous laughter made its way around the room.

"For the benefit of the rest of you, an article ran in tonight's *Times* that was . . . well, unflattering to all parties involved. I won't deny there's some truth in that story, although it is highly misleading. . . ."

From the back of the room, concealed by a large silk potted plant, Lucy watched in awe. Travis stood in front of all those people and candidly revealed the facts behind the inflammatory article. He never faltered, never shrank from the truth. She could feel the collective mood of the room subtly changing, falling under the spell of his words.

He's good, she thought, not for the first time.

"Maybe it wasn't the most politically savvy thing I've done," he acknowledged, "but I did nothing wrong, nothing I wouldn't do again tomorrow if faced with the same decision. My only mistake was in trying to conceal my involvement with the Walker-Sprague wedding."

"Didn't Nixon say the same thing?" an anonymous voice called out. Another wave of giggles rippled through the crowd.

Travis seemed to consider the heckler's question. "No, I don't think so. If he was at the wedding, he was probably on the guest list." That produced open laughter. "But seriously," he continued in the same calm, sincere tone, "I should have just told the *Times* reporter all the facts. By refusing to answer her questions, I allowed the reporter to make several untrue assumptions that have reflected badly on me as well as Leon Walker. For that, I'm truly sorry."

"All this dewy-eyed devotion is touching," came a voice in Lucy's ear. Startled, she turned to find Arthur lurking at her shoulder.

"You planned it this way, didn't you?" she accused, carefully filtering all the emotion out of her voice.

"I told you you'd be sorry you dumped me." He shrugged a negligent shoulder, making her sorry only that she hadn't considered him a real threat.

"Anyway, it was worth fifty bucks to see the look on your old man's face when he read that article."

"Which you put in his hands, no doubt."

"He'd have seen it sooner or later."

"How much did you have to pay Andrea to paint you so pretty?" Lucy asked. She didn't expect an answer to that, and she didn't get one. Instead Arthur disappeared as quietly as he'd come, like some large, slithering reptile. She shuddered, wondering how she'd overlooked this despicable side of him for so long.

"I prepared a speech for this evening," Travis was saying when she returned her attention to him, "but under the circumstances I don't think my remarks would be appropriate. Instead, I urge you to enjoy the dinner, and stay and listen to some jazz afterward."

"Are you going to withdraw from the race?" someone asked.

"I don't know," Travis replied. That was the only time his voice cracked. He left the podium then, refusing to answer questions, and headed for the exit.

Lucy followed him. He was hurting—that was obvious, despite his glib tone. The campaign was important to him, and now he'd all but lost it. She hated to think of him bearing that pain alone.

Hampered by her high heels, she didn't catch up with him until he'd reached his car. "Travis, wait."

He whirled, looking first surprised, then pleased to see her. "Lucy! I thought you left with your family."

"They tried to get me to leave with them, but I wouldn't," she explained. "I had to talk to you."

They stared at each other, Travis's car between them, and suddenly he seemed much less certain of himself. "What's left to say?" he asked.

She looked at the toes of her shoes. "I know you probably wish you'd never laid eyes on me, and I don't blame you one bit—"

"That's not true."

"Well, regardless . . . I'm really sorry everything blew up in your face. I shouldn't have involved you in the first place—"

"I involved myself, remember?"

"And I shouldn't have talked to Andrea—"

"I talked to her, too, and probably did more damage by antagonizing her than you ever could have done."

"And I definitely shouldn't have tried to get you and my father together. Look where that got you."

"I would have done it on my own anyway. Stop blaming yourself, Lucy. I made my own choices. Now I have to accept the consequences."

"It's not fair," she said miserably.

"Life's not fair." He gave a long, hopeless-sounding sigh. "Hop in, I'll give you a ride home."

She took a step backward, away from the car. "You don't have to."

"How else are you going to get home? Your ride left."

This was true, she conceded. "All right."

They both climbed into the tiny car. But instead of starting the engine, Travis leaned back in his seat and closed his eyes. She'd never seen him look so weary.

"I'm sorry I talked you into coming tonight," he said. "It was all your worst fears rolled up into one nightmarish lump, wasn't it?"

"Not the most pleasant thirty minutes of my life," she agreed. "But here I am, still alive. It didn't kill me. I figure if I can survive this, I can muddle through anything."

"Really?" The car was getting hot. He started the engine and the air conditioner. "So tonight wasn't a total loss."

She smiled weakly. "Every cloud has a silver lining, and all that garbage."

They were quiet for a time. Travis drove not toward Lucy's house, but onto the highway where he could let the Fiat eat up a few miles. The farther he got from Brennerton, the easier it was for him to look dispassionately at the scene in the banquet hall. It could have been worse, he decided. He could have been pelted with rotten tomatoes.

"You won't pull out of the race, will you?" Lucy asked in a small voice, breaking the silence.

"I don't see that I have much choice," Travis answered. "There's no point in fighting a losing battle. It would be a waste of time and money."

"But—"

"Anyway," he continued, not allowing her to object, "with the campaign behind me I can see more of you. Another silver lining." He held his breath as he waited for her response.

"I don't know," she said, dragging each word. "Haven't I...wreaked enough havoc on your life?"

He didn't answer at first. It hadn't occurred to him that Lucy might write him off. True, their association so far wasn't made in heaven. "Things almost have to get better from here, though," he observed aloud.

"But what if they get worse?"

A sobering thought. Still, as he observed Lucy's delicate profile, her fiery hair in its artfully woven style, the creamy shoulders revealed by the blue taffeta dress, and especially the slight quivering of her lower lip, he knew he couldn't walk away from her.

"We'll talk about it tomorrow," he said. By then she would have had time to realize that the end of his political career didn't mean the end of the world. Lucy had never been too keen on aligning herself with a politician. Hell, in the long run, tonight's disastrous turn of events might have been the best thing that could have happened.

Lucy rolled over in bed and burrowed under the pillows. It couldn't be morning, not yet. But the light peeking through her bedroom window confirmed that another day had dawned. Her world might be teetering on its edge, but life went on.

This was one of the rare occasions when she wasn't eager to greet a new day. All she had to look forward to was the postmortem. She wondered if it would be tactless to unplug the phone and bury herself in her work.

Her clock radio clicked on, treating her to the local radio station's weekly Saturday morning talk show. Lucy hated the show and thought the host was a ridiculous buffoon. She reached a hand out to change the station.

Her hand froze when she heard her own name. She bolted upright in bed, fully awake. What now?

"...and I just think Travis Blakeman is the most romantic personality to ever come out of Brennerton," a female call-in guest was saying. "We need a mayor with a little dash, a capacity for drama. If he can risk his career for the woman he loves..."

"What?" Lucy cried aloud as she turned up the volume.

The host took another telephone call. "I just wanted to say," came the voice of an older-sounding woman, "that you shouldn't be discussing people's personal problems over the air."

*Amen to that,* Lucy added silently.

"I'm appalled by Leon Walker's shabby behavior," the woman continued. "He should keep his politics separate from family problems. If he supported the candidate's platform yesterday, he should continue to do so today—never mind who his daughter has the hots for."

"Oh, good gravy!" Lucy wailed. But she continued to listen, fascinated. Caller after caller—most of them women—expressed admiration and support for Travis. After several minutes, she could draw only one conclusion. That horrible newspaper article, coupled with the events of last night, hadn't hurt Travis's campaign after all. Quite the contrary—the citizens of Brennerton seemed to have latched on to the romantic aspects of the story and were now casting Travis and Lucy as their town's Romeo and Juliet.

Was Travis listening? she wondered. Did he have any idea that the fickle public sentiment had taken this strange turn?

She had to call him! She leaped out of bed and ran to the phone in the kitchen, feeling suddenly energized and full of purpose. She tried him at home first, and got no answer. Then she dialed the number to his campaign office. The line was busy.

Frustrated, she hung up the phone long enough to start a pot of coffee. When she dialed again, the line was still busy. She pulled on jeans and a flowered cotton blouse, brushed her hair, put on a bit of makeup. Still, she couldn't get through.

He must be there, she decided. Perhaps he'd taken the phone off the hook, although it was hard for her to imagine him ducking phone calls. She waited five more minutes, but then her patience was at an end. She had to talk to him. He might at this very moment be withdrawing from the campaign, unaware that the tide had turned. She switched off the coffeepot and grabbed her car keys.

Travis's campaign office was in a small downtown storefront. She had to park a block away—the street was unusually congested. Was the shoe store next door having a sale? But soon she discovered the source of interest. Travis's office was packed with people.

The thought of wading through that crowd to find Travis brought a tremble to her knees. Currently she was as much an item of discussion as he, and if those people in there recognized her . . . No, she couldn't do it.

She watched through the window long enough to be sure that the mood inside the office was jovial. At one point the crowd parted and she caught a glimpse of Travis, smiling broadly. He was dressed in old jeans and a T-shirt—he obviously hadn't expected visitors.

She withdrew before she could be spotted and ambled to her car, wearing her own secret smile. By some perversity, she'd given his campaign a boost. Now she could walk away from him with a clear conscience.

Her smiled turned to a frown. That wasn't what she wanted. But when she thought back to how close she'd come to ruining his political career, she had to face the fact that she was an ill-suited match for him. A bit of notoriety hadn't changed her—she was still shy, tongue-tied Lucy Walker, afraid of crowds, paralyzed by attention. The sooner Travis disassociated himself from her, the better. Somehow she would convince him of that.

"What do you mean, no?" Travis fairly roared at her that evening. To celebrate the odd but advantageous turn of events, he'd invited her to enjoy a rare, leisurely dinner of grilled hamburgers at his town house. It was the first time she'd seen his home, and she found the grays and blues and sleek lines of his ultramodern decor attractive but oddly impersonal. She'd pegged him as the type to favor a warmer environment, and the inconsistency bothered her slightly.

Travis was bothered by another reason entirely. He'd put in ten grueling hours at the campaign office today and he felt he deserved an evening of relaxation. Unfortunately, Lucy was doing nothing to help him relax. She was strewing land mines in his path at every turn.

"Just what I said, *no,*" she replied calmly to his less-than-gentle demand. "I will not go to the Ladies' Philanthropic Society luncheon with you. Nothing has changed."

"Everything has changed," he contradicted her. "Don't you see? Now that the truth is out, we don't need to tiptoe around anymore. Everyone knows we're seeing each other. In fact, the more people see us together—" He stopped himself before verbalizing the rest of that thought, realizing how tacky it would sound. But he hadn't stopped soon enough; judging from the outraged scowl on Lucy's face, she'd finished the thought for him.

"So, now I'm a political asset, is that it? A vote getter?"

"I didn't mean that at all the way it sounded," he said with a note of apology in his voice. "I don't give a hang what people...no, that would be a baldfaced lie. Of course I care what people think. The point is, my desire to have you near me hasn't changed, regardless of public sentiment. This isn't the first time I've asked you to appear somewhere with me, is it?"

"No," she admitted.

"You're the one who insists you'll hurt my chances in the election. All I meant to do was convince you that, especially now, you're good for the campaign—" he reached out and brushed a strand of hair away from her cheek "—and good for me."

"Oh, Travis, you do have a convincing way with words," she said just before she melted against him.

God, she felt good, he thought, pressing his cheek against her silky hair. He hadn't held her in his arms like this since that night at Taluka Lake, though he'd thought about it often. He kissed the top of her head, her forehead, her cheek, and then her mouth, which welcomed him sweetly.

He resisted the urge to deepen the kiss, instead showing her all the tenderness he possessed. She meant a lot to him—too much, maybe—and he wouldn't dare risk scaring her off again. Like a timid butterfly, she was startled easily into flight. So far he'd always managed to lure her back to him. But some day he might not be able to, and that thought frightened him, even more than the prospect of losing the mayoral race.

When had she become so important to him?

"Does this mean you'll go to the luncheon?" he breathed into her ear.

"No," she whispered.

The woman was infuriatingly adamant, he mused. "Do you remember what you said last night? That if you could survive that horrible thirty minutes at the banquet you could muddle through anything?''

"Are you going to play a low politician's trick and use my own words against me?''

"Yup. Look, Lucy, I'm only asking you to try. Once. Come to one function with me. What's the worst that could happen?''

"Shall I list the possibilities in alphabetical order?'' she asked dryly. "I could knock over my water glass into your lap or flip my plate onto the floor. I could say something stupid, or blink and say nothing when someone asks me a question. I could get a chronic case of the hiccups in the middle of your speech.''

"Lucy, don't be ridiculous. Those are irrational fears. Have you ever done any of those things?''

She stepped away from him, turned, folded her arms and eyed him thoughtfully for a moment. "At the risk of scaring you, I'll go against my better judgment and make a full confession. I have done *all* of them. When I was three years old, during my church Christmas pageant, I fell off the stage into the piano. I fainted at my first communion. Once I excused myself from a dinner Dad was giving for an important supporter, and I took the tablecloth with me. I've spilled red wine down the dress of the governor's wife. And yes, once when I had to recite a poem, I threw up in front of a couple hundred parents.''

He wanted to believe she was exaggerating. He knew she wasn't. "I don't care," he said firmly.

She sighed, defeated. "All right."

"Really?" Her sudden turnabout surprised him.

"Yes, really." She'd known all along she'd say yes if he persisted. It was only yesterday that she'd promised herself she would do just that. She owed it to Travis to try to be a credit to him. She only hoped that when she failed, miserably, he wouldn't hate her.

# Chapter Eight

"It's magnificent," Lucy said after examining the printer's proof of Travis's yard signs. Because his schedule was so tight, he'd asked her to meet him at campaign headquarters, and they could ride together from there to the Ladies' Philanthropic Society luncheon. "But why didn't you put your picture on it?"

Travis groaned. "I hate to have my picture taken," he confessed. "That one they use in the paper is awful, but I haven't managed to get another one done. Anyway, I think using your picture on your campaign advertising is declassé. Just look at Wendall Cox's ads."

Lucy laughed. "That's because Wendall Cox looks like a billy goat. But in your case, it couldn't help to remind people what a handsome stud you are." She reached up and touched his cheek, one of the few times she'd been openly affectionate with him in a public place. But at that moment she felt confident enough to let the whole world know her feelings.

It couldn't be the tranquilizer, could it? She'd had a prescription for years, but she'd never taken one of the little pink pills until today. Today, however, had called for drastic measures. Her nerves had been so shattered, she'd had the choice of calling Travis and chickening out of the luncheon or numbing herself with a drug. Neither option had been to her liking.

She was about to decide she'd made the right decision after all. The tranquilizer was a mild one. She couldn't notice any difference in the way she felt, except that the butterflies in her stomach were quiet and she had a marked urge to yank Travis into the nearest dark alley and kiss him till his teeth rattled. Funny, she was sure that wasn't one of the known side effects.

Travis slipped an arm around her waist. "Are you ready?"

She gave him what felt like a dazzling smile. "If you are."

They waved goodbye to Marty Snell, Travis's campaign manager, and two volunteers who were busy on the phone.

"You seem pretty cocky today," Travis commented as he opened her car door.

"Do I?" she shot back, alarmed. "I'm not acting weird or anything, am I?"

He looked puzzled. "No. I just thought you'd be a little more . . ."

"Of a nervous wreck?" she finished for him.

"That's not exactly the way I would have put it, but you have been pretty spooked about this thing."

"Who, me?"

Travis rolled his eyes, but he was smiling as he closed her door and walked to the driver's side. "Have you talked to your father lately?" he asked once they were on their way toward Marjorie's Tea House, where the luncheon was to be held.

"As little as possible," she replied. "He must be mellowing out, though. At least, he hasn't been making any broad endorsement for Wendall."

"Thank heaven for small favors," said Travis. "Cox has enough support even without Leon."

"Ah, but you've got the women's vote." She leaned over and kissed him on the cheek. He actually seemed embarrassed at all the attention she was giving him, which caused her to wonder once again if she was behaving strangely. "You would tell me if I was making a fool of myself, wouldn't you?'' she asked impulsively.

He cast her a sly, sideways glance. "You can make a fool of yourself with me any day, and I won't complain.''

"Travis, I'm serious.''

He shook his head, apparently not getting the drift of her concern, but he placed a reassuring hand on her knee and left it there during the remainder of the short drive, a gentle reminder that they were on the same side.

The luncheon was in the party room at Marjorie's, a Victorian mansion converted into a restaurant. It had only opened a few months earlier. Lucy had never been there, although Sandy and Judy both raved about it.

Though the meeting room was large, the Ladies' Philanthropic Society had a lot of members crowded into it. Several of the woman, mostly grandmotherly types, rushed up to greet Travis and Lucy as soon as they arrived. There was one man present, too—the beady-eyed *Times* reporter, who apparently had been assigned to shadow Travis during the campaign. Travis gave him a discreet nod of acknowledgment.

"We're so glad you could make it, Mr. Blakeman,'' said Vernie Lowery, the group's president. "And you too, Miss Walker.'' She turned to two of her friends. "Don't they make a cute couple? So tell me, have you set the date yet?"

Lucy turned terrified eyes to Travis.

"Um, no," he said quickly, sounding ill at ease for the first time since she had known him. "We're not engaged."

"You don't say?" Vernie pursed her lips. "I thought you were."

It was no wonder people got the wrong idea, Lucy thought with mounting distress. Ever since the fund-raising dinner, rumors about them had flown thick and fast.

"Well, there's time enough for that after you're elected," Vernie concluded, deftly smoothing over the awkward moment. "Let me introduce you around. Would you like something cold to drink before lunch?"

"Tea, please," Lucy said immediately. Her mouth was as dry as the August sun-parched grass outside.

Vernie seemed pleased with Lucy's choice. "Just the thing on a day like today. They do make such wicked tea here." She dispatched the waitress to bring a glass of Marjorie's signature drink, as well as the ice water Travis had requested.

Reluctantly, Lucy allowed herself to be drawn away from Travis and into a throng of younger women, all of whom seemed to be fascinated by her. They were polite but curious, and the more brief her

answers to their questions became the more inquis-
itive they got.

She knew they were only trying to make her feel
at home, but there was no way she could feel comfortable when six people were staring at her, hanging on her every word, no matter how sparse those
words were. What was worse, the room was sti-
fling. She could feel perspiration trickling down the
back of her neck and between her breasts.

Somehow she managed. When her iced tea arrived a few minutes later she was so relieved to have
a distraction that she gulped down half the glass. It
was only when she slowed down that she noticed
how odd the brew tasted. Delicious, but different.
Must be some obscure blend, she decided.

"Do you wear furs?" one of the women asked
abruptly.

"No, but—"

"Oh, thank heavens," another said. "Are you in
favor of recycling?"

"It's really not my place to—"

"Oh, but it is, Lucy. A mayor's wife has so much
influence—"

Lucy choked. Someone handed her a fresh glass
of iced tea. She took several swallows. "Thank
you," she said when her windpipe was clear again.
"And I'm not Travis's wife, not even close," she
said firmly. "My views are my own, and they have
nothing to do with him." She was proud of the fact

that she managed to say that much. If Travis insisted on including her at political functions, the least she could do was to minimize any possible damage a careless word on her part could do.

"But what *do* you think of recycling?" the woman persisted, though somewhat hesitantly. "I mean, just as a regular person?"

Lucy smiled. "I'm recycling aluminum and newspapers myself—what about you?"

The woman never had a chance to answer, as Vernie picked that moment to announce that lunch was served and everyone should take their chairs. Relieved, Lucy hurried to the head table and her seat beside Travis. Her head was spinning from all the chatter she'd been subjected to.

Travis leaned down and whispered in her ear, "How's it going so far?"

"Not too well," she said, and took another sip of her drink. "I wish they would turn the air-conditioning up."

"You better take it easy on that stuff," he cautioned.

"What, this?" She shook the ice in her almost-empty glass. "It's just iced tea."

His eyes widened. "Lucy, that's Long Island tea. Marjorie's stakes its claim to fame on the stuff. I thought you knew that."

She shrugged. Did it matter where the tea came from?

"It's made from at least four different kinds of liquor," he persisted when she didn't get his point. "It'll knock you on your tush faster than you can blink."

"Oh. Ooh." No wonder her head was spinning. Two glasses of the stuff on top of a tranquilizer— oh, hell. "Travis, I think maybe I ought to excuse myself."

"What? Why?"

"Because when that tea hits me, it won't be a pretty sight." She was afraid to tell him about the tranquilizer.

He peered into her eyes, concern etched into his every facial muscle. "How do you feel now?"

"All right, I guess." She straightened her back and reconsidered her decision to flee. "Yes, I'm fine. Maybe if I eat some of this bread . . ."

Travis cut a piece off the small sourdough loaf in front of them and buttered it for her. "Are you sure?"

"Yes, really." She gave him a reassuring smile. She would *not* spoil the whole afternoon by asking him to take her home. She felt relaxed and a little light-headed, that was all.

A waiter came by and placed huge plates of tuna salad in front of them. Travis was allowed only a few bites before he was invited to the podium to speak. Lucy, not overly fond of tuna anyway, only picked at hers.

She listened raptly to Travis speak, delighted with the way he seemed to so effortlessly charm the group of women. But somewhere about halfway through the speech, his words began to run together in her mind, making no sense at all, and she lost all feeling in her fingers and toes. She thought about leaving the room, but somehow she lacked the ability to do so. Then, mercifully, someone turned out the lights.

Travis felt on top of the world. This was a fun group. They already liked him, so they were easy to entertain. What made things especially pleasurable for him, however, was that he could look over at Lucy every few minutes and see her encouraging smile. He could get used to having her with him all the time, he mused as he paused to take a sip of water.

He glanced over at her just before he began his closing remarks—and his heart stopped. "Lucy!" Her name reverberated throughout the room, and yet she didn't move.

He was at her side instantly, scooping her into his arms carrying her to a Victorian settee in the hallway outside the meeting room. One of the women, a retired nurse, came forward to help. She opened the top two buttons of Lucy's dress and bathed her face and neck with cold water. Another woman produced a vial of smelling salts.

To Travis's immense relief, Lucy came to as soon as she got a whiff of the salts. She jerked her head up and pushed the offending vial out of her face, then looked around her with huge, bewildered eyes. "What happened?"

"You fainted," the nurse said. "No, don't try to sit up yet." She folded a wet napkin and instructed Lucy to hold it against her forehead. "You'll be all right in a minute or two. It was so hot in that room, I'm surprised we're not all dropping like flies."

Silently Travis blessed the woman for saying just the right thing. No one mentioned Long Island tea. He turned toward Vernie and the other concerned women hovering in the hallway, then nodded toward Lucy. "Could we have a few minutes?"

"Of course, Mr. Blakeman," said Vernie, ushering the other ladies away.

When they were alone, he knelt beside the settee and took Lucy's hand in his. "How do you feel?"

"Wretched. Like cannons are exploding behind my eyes and a herd of wildebeests is stampeding my stomach." She sat up slowly, despite his protests. "Travis?"

"Yes, sweetheart, what is it?"

"Why do I have mayonnaise in my hair?"

He sat beside her, putting his arm around her shoulders. She felt suddenly small and fragile. "You, um, took a nosedive into your tuna salad."

"Oh, no." She buried her face in her hands. When next she spoke, her words were strangled with tears. "I gave you fair warning, Travis, but you just didn't believe me."

He pulled her against his shoulder. "Lucy, sweetheart, it's not your fault."

"Of course it's my f-fault. This is who and what I am, Travis. You have to face that."

"I know exactly who and what you are," he said softly. "You could pass out into a hundred plates of tuna salad and it wouldn't make any difference to me. I love you, and *you* have to face *that*."

She raised her head and stared at him as if he'd just announced he wanted to move to New Guinea and start a rutabaga farm. Well, he couldn't blame her. He hadn't intended to blurt it out like that. Hell, he'd only just realized himself how deeply his feelings ran.

He waited. She didn't offer any reciprocal sentiments, but at least she'd stopped crying.

"Think you can walk?" he asked when the long silence threatened to become awkward.

She nodded mutely.

"I'll just tell the ladies goodbye and take you home."

Lucy sat on the settee as he disappeared into the meeting room, grateful that the excruciating physical sensations had dulled to a merely disconcerting numbness. On an emotional level, however, she was anything but numb.

Travis had just said he loved her. *Loved* her, after she'd fallen face-first into her lunch and embarrassed the tar out of him as well as herself. Maybe he'd had a few swigs of that wicked tea himself. Something ought to account for his temporary insanity. And that was all it was, she was sure—a temporary urge to say something, anything, to stop her from crying. Men were funny about women's tears.

Still, she wished he hadn't said the words. He was only making things harder.

She sat stiffly beside him on the way home. Travis, on the other hand, chattered like a parrot, trying to reassure her that she had nothing to be embarrassed about, that Vernie and the other ladies were full of understanding and compassion.

"What about that reporter?" she asked, speaking for the first time since she'd climbed into the car. "He didn't looked like the compassionate type to me."

Travis shrugged. "Guess we'll find out when we get tomorrow's paper."

Lucy groaned. How could he be so nonchalant about it?

He pulled into her driveway and assisted her out of the car, for which she was grateful. She still felt weak as a baby bird. But she didn't allow him through the front door. She stood in the doorway, blocking his entry with unmistakable intent.

"I'm really sorry, Travis."

"You don't have to apologize. Are you sure you'll be all right?"

"Positive," she lied. "You can go."

"Your car is still downtown," he reminded her. "Why don't you give me the keys and I'll bring it over later tonight?"

She waved her hand in a dismissive gesture. "I can get it. I'm sure you have more important things to do."

He looked at her uncertainly. "I'll call you later, then, and see how you're—"

"Please don't."

He stared at her, uncomprehending.

"I can't handle the pressure anymore, Travis," she said, using the words she'd mentally rehearsed on the way home. "If I see my name in print or hear it on the radio one more time I'll...I'll go crazy. I'm a nervous wreck as it is. I can't even walk down the street without someone pointing at me and whispering. I was so agitated over this stupid luncheon today that I took a tranquilizer for the first time in my life. I can't handle things anymore."

When she saw the pain those words caused in his velvety brown eyes, she wished she could take them back. Almost. They weren't exactly the truth. But they were the only words that would make him see reason.

If it were merely a matter of her own discomfort, her own anxiety, she could bear it. But she would not continue to discredit him. He was kind and understanding about it now, but what about the next time she embarrassed him as she had today? Or the time after that? What if she cost him the election?

Understanding would turn to resentment soon enough. And she didn't think she could bear to see the affection in his gaze fade into irritation, or worse.

"Let me come in," he said after a few moments. "Let's talk about it."

"No. I won't change my mind. Goodbye, Travis." She closed the door on him, blocking his face from her view, but she knew she'd remember his agonized expression for a long, long time to come.

Three days passed and he didn't call, though everyone else did. A hideously embarrassing account of the luncheon in the paper prompted concerned calls from both her sisters, her mother and various friends, all of them seeking reassurance that she wasn't truly ill. She gave them that, but volunteered no further information. She wasn't in the mood to talk to anyone.

It was good Travis hadn't called, she tried to tell herself, because no matter how persuasive he became, she wouldn't have changed her mind this time. Rejecting him was the hardest thing she'd ever done; why would she want to prolong the process?

But she craved the sound of his voice, and some perverse part of her was disappointed he'd given up so easily.

"Well, what did you expect?" she asked herself aloud as she fixed lunch, a grilled cheese sandwich that she didn't really want. When you slam a door in a guy's face, that doesn't leave him much encouragement.

Another hour of silence drove her near the edge; she had to get out. After gathering up enough work to keep her busy for awhile no matter where she went, she headed for her car.

She'd go to her parents' house. She'd hardly been civil to them since the fund-raising dinner, and maybe it was time she made peace. They, at least, would be happy that she and Travis had parted company. But instead of turning toward the house, she maneuvered her car onto the highway and headed for the Hide-Away Lodge. She didn't stop to analyze her motives.

She found Nan Blakeman seated at the registration desk, playing a desultory game of solitaire. Nan looked up and her face brightened when she saw Lucy.

"Well, hi there, darlin'," Nan said, standing as she pushed the forgotten cards aside. "I was hoping you two might stop by. I've been trying to get hold of Travis—where is he?"

"It's...it's just me this time," Lucy said. "Travis and I—we aren't seeing each other."

Nan's hand flew to her mouth to stifle a gasp. "What did that dumb-bunny brother of mine do this time? I swear, every time he finds a nice girl—"

"It's not his fault," Lucy interrupted. "It's me—I mean, mine. My fault." She took a deep breath and tried to compose her thoughts. What was it she wanted to say?

Nan shook her head. "Lucy, darlin', it's never the woman's fault. Don't you know the rules?"

"Rules?"

"Come on, let's go make some coffee—no, tea with lemon," Nan said with an encouraging smile. "You can tell me all about it."

Lucy did just that. She stumbled through the story, making several false starts, but eventually she got it told, emphasizing her distress rather than her fears for Travis's career. Nan listened without interrupting, though a small frown of disapproval stole across her face as she gradually came to understand the circumstances.

"So why did you come here?" Nan said bluntly.

"I don't know. Maybe I just wanted to find out how he's doing . . ." Lucy's voice trailed off.

"I haven't talked to him," Nan said. "Maybe I'll just give him a call right now." She made a move for the phone, but Lucy stopped her.

"No, please, don't call him. I don't want him to know I'm here."

Nan halted, then reclaimed her stool and appraised Lucy with a cool eye. "Sounds to me like you've got it bad, kiddo. You look like hell—if you don't mind my being blunt—and if you ask me, you're putting yourself through a lot more misery than a few lousy public appearances would bring. What you're really worried about is embarrassing him, isn't it?"

"Yes," Lucy answered, knowing it was useless to lie. Nan, for all her down-home friendliness, was as shrewd as they come.

"Listen, my brother is a big boy. Why don't you worry about making Lucy happy, and let him worry about his public image?"

"Because he refuses to worry about it, that's why," Lucy said, suddenly vehement. "He thinks he can mold me into the kind of woman he wants and needs, and it just won't work. I'm trying to save us both a lot of heartbreak."

If Nan had looked disapproving before, her sharply lowered eyebrows now spelled outright condemnation.

"I just want you to understand," Lucy mumbled, not sure what she'd done wrong.

"Well, you can save the martyr act. All my life I've waited for a man to be as crazy about me as Travis is about you, and it's never happened. So don't expect me to feel sorry for you because you're tossing it away."

Lucy was so shocked at Nan's sudden animosity, she could think of nothing to say in response. If she'd come here looking for a shoulder to cry on, she'd obviously looked in the wrong place. "Well, of course your sympathies are with your brother," she finally said.

"I'm not taking sides," Nan said gruffly. "I'd like to see you both happy. And I'm sorry if I sounded rude or hateful, but I don't mince words."

Lucy accepted Nan's apology, awkwardly gulped down the rest of her tea and left as quickly as she decently could. Nan's harsh words had left her feeling raw and uneasy. It wasn't that she wanted or deserved sympathy. She'd come to the Hide-Away Lodge with the hope that Nan would be able to reassure her that Travis was getting along all right, that's all. But she hadn't expected to get a lecture.

She fell back on her original plan and drove to her parents' house. The front gates were open, so she was able to slip into the house unnoticed. Gwen was probably home, but Lucy wasn't yet ready to talk to her mother. She donned a swimsuit she kept in the closet of her old room, grabbed a handful of manuscript pages she'd brought with her, and found a shady spot by the pool. Maybe she could find peace there, by the cool blue water.

She forced her concentration onto her work, copy editing a textbook on statistics. It was boring as all get out—much worse than the *Arachnid Journal*. But at least she found a certain amount of satisfaction in molding the text to her will, turning dull semantics and bad grammar into clear, lively narrative. If only her own life were so easy to manipulate.

Gwen, dressed in her chic gardening attire and designer gloves, found her a couple of hours later. "Gracious, I didn't know you were here—Lucy, darling, are you all right?"

"No. As a matter of fact, I'm dreadful."

"You're not ill, are you?" Gwen sat in an adjacent chair and brushed her daughter's hair from her face, as she'd done when Lucy was a child. "It's Travis, then, isn't it? Now that your father's support is out of the question, he's dropped you like a hot potato."

Anger welled up inside Lucy at her mother's glib assumption. She banged her hands against the glass tabletop, causing Gwen to jump in surprise. "No, Mother, that's not it at all. I'm the one who did the dropping. Dad's support or lack of it has nothing to do with Travis and me. Why won't you believe that?''

Gwen appeared taken aback by Lucy's sudden outburst. "If that's true, then what *did* happen between you two?"

"I thought you'd be the first to figure it out," Lucy said in a calmer tone, settling back into her chair. "You did warn me, after all."

"I did?"

"That I wouldn't mix well with a politician. The public appearances, the press coverage, all that attention . . ."

Gwen was nodding. "The pressure was too much for you. Is that why you fainted at the luncheon?"

"That, plus a tranquilizer and two Long Island teas. I fell face-first into my tuna salad," Lucy confessed. "At least the *Times* didn't print that part."

"Oh, Lucy." Gwen shook her head wistfully. "You do have a talent for putting on a good show."

"Unfortunately it's not the sort of talent that's useful at this stage in my life. I wish I could be more like you." When she saw the surprised look on her mother's face, she realized she'd never said that aloud before. "It's true. You always say and do the right things. You're the perfect politician's wife, and I'm . . . a walking disaster." The last few words came out on a moan.

Lucy expected her mother to comfort her, as she'd always done in situations like this. But instead Gwen sat very still, not even reaching a hand out to touch her daughter. She stared over the swimming pool, unseeing, with a pensive look on her face.

"You know, Lucy," she said after a few more silent moments, "I might have been wrong about something. When I said you weren't well suited to be in the public eye, those were careless words. I wouldn't have said them if I'd had any idea your feelings for Travis ran so deep."

"It was only the truth," Lucy said glumly.

"Not necessarily. I won't deny that my outgoingness and my love for entertaining have made me an asset to your father's career, but there are other ways to achieve the same end."

"What do you mean?"

Gwen studied her daughter again, as if seeing her for the first time. "There's something about you... something about the way Travis Blakeman reacts to you that makes you very appealing as a couple."

"Oh, Mother, don't be ridiculous!"

"No, I'm serious. You've already parlayed a few embarrassing incidents into spectacular publicity for Travis. And you're not without some assets, after all. You're pretty, and you can be very charming when you open that mouth of yours."

"When I don't put my foot in it," Lucy grumbled.

"Darling, listen to what I'm saying. You're shy and everyone knows it. Why fight it? Capitalize on it. It did wonders for Princess Diana. As for your occasional, uh, clumsiness when you get nervous? Look at President Ford. He was always tripping, bumping his head, and everyone loved it."

Lucy groaned. What a ridiculous argument, comparing her to princesses and presidents. "It's a moot point anyway," she said. "Travis and I are finished. He'll be much better off without me."

Gwen sighed impatiently. "All right, if you insist on being a martyr..."

*A martyr!* Why was everyone calling her that?

"I *am* going to talk to your father, by the way," Gwen said. "We just assumed Travis was using you to get to Leon, but I'm beginning to see that's not the case."

For the first time in three days, Lucy felt a glimmer of optimism. Her father could still help Travis win the election, and all this heartache would at least have had a purpose. "Oh, Mother, I wish you would."

"I'll do what I can," Gwen said, ruffling Lucy's hair affectionately. "As for you—" She was interrupted by the housekeeper's approach. "Yes, Ruth, what is it?"

"There's a phone call for Lucy," Ruth said.

Lucy frowned. Who knew she was here? She rushed across the patio and through the French doors to the kitchen, hoping irrationally that Travis had tracked her down. But it was a woman's voice that greeted her.

"Lucy, I'm so glad I found you. This is Nan. I'm ... I'm sorry I yelled at you. I had no call to do that."

"It's okay," Lucy said. "I know you didn't mean it unkindly."

"Good, I'm glad you understand," Nan said briskly. "Now, the real reason I called—oh, Lucy, you've got to do something. Marty, Travis's campaign manager, just called. Travis is pulling the plug on the campaign."

"You mean he's—"

"Quitting," Nan finished for her. "He's holding a press conference at four o'clock at the River Inn to announce that he's withdrawing. He says the campaign is ruining his love life."

# Chapter Nine

"No. Oh, no, he can't *do* this," Lucy shrieked. "I have to stop him." She looked at her watch. It was three forty-five. "Thank you, Nan, thank you for telling me. I have to go." She hung up and dashed out of the kitchen as Gwen looked on in amazement.

She took the long, curved staircase two steps at a time. When she reached her old bedroom, where she'd donned the swimsuit, she began throwing on her clothes willy-nilly, again cursing her wardrobe. She'd worn jeans and a T-shirt sporting a soft-drink logo. Would they even let her into the River Inn?

"Remind me to buy new clothes," she told her mother as she passed her on the staircase.

"Lucy, what's this all— Lucy!"

Lucy ignored the calls. She didn't have a minute to waste.

It was precisely four o'clock when she reached the River Inn, after breaking every traffic law on the books. She abandoned her car at the front door and rushed inside, only to wander around frantically until someone directed her to the right room.

She peeked inside and discovered a comfortingly small crowd—just a reporter and photographer from the paper, a similar pair of TV journalists and someone from the local radio station. A couple of young women, probably from the student newspaper at the nearby university, completed the cast.

Travis had just stood to take the podium. Before he had a chance to begin his announcement, she opened the door wide and walked in. Every head in the room swiveled to stare at her. Travis's jaw dropped.

"Excuse me," she mumbled as she ducked her head and strode purposefully toward the front of the room. She tried not to think about all the eyes following her. She had a mission to accomplish, and nothing was going to stop her.

Travis took two steps away from the podium to meet her, still fighting the shock of her presence. She was the last person he'd expected to see, but he was glad she'd come. He was doing this for her, after all.

He grasped her hands in greeting, resisting the urge to grab her and kiss her in front of the room full of reporters. "What are you doing here?" he asked.

"I have to talk to you," she whispered, a note of urgency in her voice.

"In just a minute we can talk all you want," he whispered back. "I've figured out how to solve everything."

He started to return to the podium. Lucy grabbed him by the tie and jerked him back. A strobe went off, but Travis could only smile at the thought of the photo that would appear in tomorrow's paper. Embarrassing publicity couldn't hurt him any longer.

Lucy, still holding on to his tie, pulled him down to her level. "I have to talk to you *now*," she said fiercely.

He held his hands up in a gesture of surrender. "All right, all right. You don't have to get violent. Marty," he said to his campaign manager, who was looking on with frank interest, "Lucy and I are going next door for a moment. Please ask the reporters to be patient awhile longer."

As they stepped through a door into an empty, adjacent meeting room, they could hear Marty making an apology.

The moment the door was closed, Lucy turned on Travis like a cornered bobcat. "You will *not* withdraw from the mayor's race, do you hear me? I won't stand for it.''

Travis was shocked and a little amused at her ferocity. "What are you going to do about it?'' he asked, crossing his arms and leaning against the wall.

"I'll...I don't know. All I know is I will not be responsible for your throwing away your political career.''

Seeing how distressed she was, he dropped his teasing. "You're not responsible. I'm the one who's withdrawing. I've thought it over very carefully. I meant what I said the other day, Lucy. I love you. Being with you means more to me than any campaign possibly could. So let me go out there and make my announcement, and then we can...I don't know. Go to a movie or something. Date. Act like real people. I could even spend the night at your house and no one would care.''

But she was shaking her head. "Oh, Travis, it won't work. You're a gifted leader, an honest one— something we don't see every day. This town needs you. And who knows, you could end up on the state legislature, or even in congress. I couldn't live with myself, knowing I was the cause of your giving up a career you were meant for.''

"I don't believe this! The other day you gave me the boot because my political career is too tough on your nerves. And now you're telling me that even if I quit politics you still won't see me?"

"I guess that's what I'm saying." She bit down on her lower lip and looked everywhere but at him.

"Then there's nothing I can do?"

She shook her head miserably.

He stuck his hands in his pockets. "Well, then, I guess—" He cut himself off as an inspiration hit him. There was one thing he could do. It was a pretty dirty trick, but she gave him no choice—no choice at all. He was a desperate man.

"You guess what?" Lucy asked.

"I guess I won't withdraw from the race."

She looked infinitely relieved. "Thank goodness you're being sensible."

"On one condition," he added.

"What condition?" she asked warily.

"Marry me."

Her jaw dropped and her eyes grew as large and round as two silver dollars. "You're crazy, you know that?"

"Those are my terms," he said calmly, though he was a sheer mass of nerves below the surface. "You agree to marry me, and I'll continue to campaign. Say no, and..."

"No!"

He shrugged. "Okay." He turned nonchalantly and reached for the door.

"Wait."

He paused, holding his breath.

"Two months ago, when I told you you needed to learn how to get in the trenches and fight dirty, I didn't mean with me. You've put me in a terrible position."

He smiled mischievously. "I know."

"Damn you! All right, I'll marry you." She folded her arms and stared defiantly at him, her eyes twin flames of green fire.

"A week from Saturday."

She opened her mouth to object, then seemed to think better of it. He had her over a barrel and she knew it. "Whenever you say." Her words were soft and deadly. "But come November you better get elected or I'll kill you."

Well, better a murderous fiancée than no fiancée at all, he reasoned. He came toward her, arms out-stretched. "Lucy, sweetheart—"

"Don't 'sweetheart' me until you go in there and cancel that press conference."

He gave her a mock salute and a cocky smile, and secretly hoped he'd been justified in employing such extreme measures. He wouldn't have done it if he didn't believe she loved him. He'd feel better, though, if she would just say the words.

She stood in the corner of the room and refused to come near him as he returned to the podium. "It appears I've made a slight miscalculation," he told the small assemblage of reporters and photographers. "The announcement I planned to make is now null and void. I apologize for any inconvenience this might have caused you." He started to step away.

"Wait a minute," an indignant reporter called out. "I thought you were going to withdraw from the campaign."

"A nasty rumor," Travis replied easily. But he tensed when he saw Lucy edging her way toward the door. He wanted to announce to the reporters, to the whole world, for that matter, that he and Lucy were getting married, but if he took the time to do that he'd lose the opportunity to follow her. "That's all the questions for now," he concluded hastily before tailing her out of the room.

"Where are you off to?" he said as he followed her across the hotel lobby.

"Where do you think?" she replied acidly. "I'm going home to make wedding plans."

"Lucy!" He caught hold of her arm and forced her to stand still and face him. "You don't hate me for trumping your ace, do you?"

She gave an exasperated sigh. "No, I could never hate you. But I'm very, very angry right now."

"You cornered me. I fight mean when I'm cornered."

"So I've discovered."

"I wouldn't hold you to it if I didn't think you loved me," he said softly.

"I do," she said, her eyes downcast. But when she looked up at him again, her face was filled with determination. "If I didn't love you, I wouldn't bother waiting till the campaign is over. I'd just shoot you now and be done with it."

Illogically, he laughed. "My shy, timid, quiet Lucy. Where did you get such a temper?"

"From my father, of course," she replied easily. "And while we're on the subject of him, what are your plans for Sunday night?"

"I . . . um, don't think I have any, for a change."

"Good. Pick me up at six. We're having dinner at my folks' house, and you can join me in making our little announcement. I'd hate to be greedy and hoard that privilege all to myself."

Travis gulped. He hadn't thought that far ahead—actually facing Leon Walker again, and as his daughter's prospective bridegroom. "Should I wear my bulletproof vest?" he asked.

She seemed to consider this. "I don't think that's necessary, but an asbestos suit might be useful. I'd definitely expect fireworks."

Gwen was the perfect hostess at Sunday's family dinner, smiling and accommodating; Lucy's sisters and their husbands were talkative, happily including Travis in their conversation as they enjoyed cocktails on the patio. Even Leon remained pleasant, though he confined his comments to sports and the weather.

Where *were* the fireworks? Lucy wondered. Why were they being so nice? Was there still hope for harmony in this family?

After a satisfying meal of stuffed pork chops, mashed potatoes and peas, followed by chocolate bundt cake, the mood was still so amicable that she hated to rock the boat. But the time had come to make the announcement.

She waited for a lull in the conversation, cleared her throat and took a deep breath. "Travis and I have an announcement to make," she said with a sideways glance toward him. He gave her an encouraging smile. "We're g-getting, uh…getting…" The word slipped her mind.

"Married," Travis supplied.

The ensuing silence was profound. Had she just lit the fuse? she wondered. Then, suddenly, the table seemed to explode as everyone talked at once. Lucy found herself scooped up into one hug after another, and Travis received handshakes, back slaps and kisses on the cheek. Only her father held back, offering neither approval nor disapproval.

"When?" her mother finally asked.

"This Saturday," Lucy answered.

"What?" Gwen shrieked, and her normally unshakable composure slipped dramatically. "How do you expect me to plan a wedding in less than a week? There's invitations and flowers to order—we probably can't even get the church. This just won't do. I'll need three months, minimum.''

''Don't worry, Mother, you won't have to lift a finger. I don't expect you and Dad to spring for another wedding. This one's on me. I'm planning to ask Judge Hadley to perform the ceremony in his chambers. All the rest of you need to do is show up.''

Gwen shuddered. ''Oh, Lucy, you can't. No daughter of mine is getting married at a courthouse. What will the papers have to say about that?''

''The papers won't know, because the ceremony is top secret. Only immediate family is invited. I'm counting on every one of you to keep your mouths shut. Promise me now—you won't interfere, or I swear we'll elope. I have no intention of letting this thing get out of hand like it did last time.''

The mention of her calamitous near-wedding with Arthur cast a pall of silence over the table.

Abruptly, Leon stood and announced it was time for brandy and cigars. He gave Travis a pointed look.

So, Lucy thought, a few fireworks were still on the program. She exchanged a worried look with Travis just before he followed her father to the library, looking like a lamb being led to slaughter.

When Leon closed the library doors, Travis was disconcerted to discover that Charlie and Don had opted out of the after-dinner tradition. *They must be squeamish at the sight of blood,* he concluded.

Leon poured two fingers of brandy from a crystal decanter into two snifters, then offered one to Travis. Travis, never fond of brandy, took it anyway.

"Why don't you sit down, Blakeman?" Leon suggested as he settled into his worn leather chair.

Travis did, gratefully. The way his knees were shaking, he couldn't have remained standing much longer.

"So, you want to marry my daughter."

"Yes, sir." For the first time in his life, Travis felt tongue-tied. Now he had an inkling of understanding for the torture Lucy often endured.

"All I've ever wanted for my girls is to see them happy," Leon said. "Sandy and Judy—I never worried much about them. They had men bearing down on them from all directions. All they had to do was pick and choose the best. Lucy, now—Lucy's different. I worry about her. She needs someone who understands her and can take care of her."

"Begging your pardon, sir," Travis said, amazed at his own boldness, "but I disagree. Lucy takes very good care of herself. What she needs is someone to push her into facing the things she's afraid of. She's capable of much more than anyone gives her credit for.''

Leon seemed to think about this. ''I'll grant that she does seem a bit more sure of herself since you came on the scene,'' he said. ''But she'll always be shy. A leopard can't change its spots, you know. Your career will be hard on her.''

''I know that. I also know she'll be a credit to me.''

''Do you love her?'' Leon asked point-blank.

Travis had no trouble answering that question. ''Yes. I was prepared to give up the politics for her, but she wouldn't let me.''

Leon nodded thoughtfully. ''So that's what that ridiculous press conference was all about. I wondered.'' He set the smoldering cigar in an ashtray, rose from his chair and wandered over to his heavy, ornately carved desk. ''Blakeman ... Travis,'' he corrected himself. ''I was convinced you were nothing but a crass opportunist. But my wife seems to think otherwise, and she's pretty savvy about these things. I usually follow her instincts. Unfortunately, you've put me in a very delicate position. I publicly supported you, then just as publicly denounced you. If I reverse myself again, the people of Brennerton will think I have a cog loose.''

''I understand that. I'm not counting on your support. All I'm asking is that you let Lucy know that you don't mind her marrying me, that's all.''

Leon smiled. "Well, I think I can swing that, and perhaps a bit more." He reached into his desk drawer, pulled out a piece of paper and handed it to Travis. "You're not to tell a soul where you got that," he said.

With a start, Travis realized he'd just accepted a check made out to his campaign fund—one with a lot of zeroes. The check had been made out in advance. Leon had planned to support Travis even before Lucy announced the upcoming marriage.

"Why?" Travis asked, somewhat bewildered.

"Because your opponent is a braying jackass. And I *like* your politics, son. Just don't tell anyone I told you that. As far as anyone will know, when it comes to the Brennerton mayor's race, I am now officially neutral."

Saturday dawned crisp and clear, cool for early September and utterly perfect for a wedding. Lucy, however, wasn't thinking about the weather. In her parents' plush bedroom suite, she was experiencing an eerie sense of déjà vu as she dressed for the ceremony, with her mother and sisters attending.

She was nervous, there was no denying that. Her hands trembled so violently that it took three attempts to get her mascara on without smearing it all over her face.

"Don't worry, you're supposed to have the jitters," Sandy assured her as she steamed nonexistent wrinkles out of the simple white linen suit Lucy had bought for the occasion. "You wouldn't be a normal bride if you weren't a little nervous."

"A little?" said Lucy. "I tried to put my bra on backward."

"But you aren't nearly the wreck you were last time," Judy argued as she removed hot rollers from Lucy's hair. "Oops, I forgot, we weren't supposed to mention the last time."

Gwen sat on the edge of the bed, watching the preparations. "Well, I, for one, do need to say something about the *other* wedding."

Lucy inwardly cringed. Gwen had spoken very little about the approaching nuptials over the past week. Now she probably was going to air her disapproval over the painfully simple ceremony Lucy had arranged.

"Lucy, sweetheart, I want to apologize for what your sisters and I did with the other wedding."

"What?" Lucy couldn't help saying.

"We railroaded you into a wedding that was completely inappropriate for you. I refused to consider your shyness, or how uncomfortable you would be. I was more interested in how the ceremony would be written up in the paper than I was on launching your marriage. But now that I've watched you plan your own wedding, I can see this is how it should have been all along—an intimate, tasteful ceremony."

"We're sorry, too," Sandy added, as Judy nodded enthusiastically.

Lucy was so moved, she couldn't get any words past her constricted throat. Gwen seldom admitted to making a mistake, and Lucy knew what the apology had cost her. She went to her mother and wrapped her arms around her neck.

Gwen gingerly returned the hug. "Careful, honey, you'll muss your hair."

"I can always fix it again," Lucy said. "Oh, Mother, you don't have to apologize. If you hadn't thrown that gargantuan wedding, I never would have jumped out the window, and then Travis and I might never have gotten together."

"That's one way to look at it," Gwen agreed, finally surrendering to the hug and squeezing her daughter unmercifully for a few seconds before releasing her.

When her family pronounced her ready, she appraised herself in her mother's gilt-edged full-length mirror. This time she liked what she saw. She looked like a bride—happy, flushed with excitement, not grim and sickly pale.

"Oh! We almost forgot the hat," Judy said, fetching a singularly unattractive pillbox hat from a box on the bed.

Lucy grimaced, but she allowed them to position and pin it on her head. She hadn't wanted to wear a hat, but Gwen had paled at the thought of Lucy marrying bareheaded, so Lucy had given in to this one concession.

"It's beautiful," she managed, even as she prayed that no one would remember a camera.

A few minutes later she was riding to the courthouse in her parents' Lincoln with Judy and Charlie, while Sandy and Don followed in their car. Though she clutched her bouquet, a small cluster of camellias, in a death grip, she was far more calm than she would have thought possible.

Leon made an exasperated noise. "I can't find a parking place. What are all these people doing downtown on a Saturday, anyway?"

"It must be that Saturday traffic court they started," Gwen answered sensibly. "Why don't you drop us off out front, dear."

Lucy looked out the window. "You mean we're here already?" But there was the courthouse, a great architectural monstrosity with about a million steps leading up to its boxy facade.

"Hey, you're holding up great, Sis," Judy said as they scooted out of the back seat.

"There is *nothing* to worry about," Gwen insisted as Charlie opened the double glass doors and admitted them all to the cool courthouse interior.

Lucy was almost ready to believe that as her eyes adjusted to the light. That's when she realized that the courthouse was crawling with people—all of them staring and pointing at her.

## Chapter Ten

"There she is," someone cried. Before Lucy could react, a half-dozen flashes of light temporarily blinded her. Then all around her were murmurs of, "That's her," and, "There's the bride."

For several heartbeats she was paralyzed, rooted to the granite floor like a small redwood. An intrusive light from a television camera hit her in the face as a toothy reporter stepped closer.

Gwen came to the rescue. Eschewing her normal public persona, she fairly growled at the reporter like a lioness protecting her cub. "Would you get out of my daughter's face?" she barked. "Go find a nice natural disaster somewhere in another state."

Lucy took advantage of the momentary distraction her mother's outburst caused and bolted—ran as fast as her cursed linen pumps would allow across the rotunda on a direct route toward the ladies' room, pushing aside any curious onlookers who chanced to block her path. She didn't stop, not for anything, until she'd burst through the swinging door and careened into one of the stalls. Without bothering to lock the stall door, she unceremoniously lost her breakfast.

Frantic footsteps followed her into the bathroom. "Luce? Are you all right?" It was Judy.

"What do you think?" Lucy replied on a moan, pressing her face against the cool metal of the stall divider. "Just don't let anyone in here. I couldn't bear to pick up the Sunday paper and read about myself throwing up before my wedding." She teetered out of the stall and to the sink, rinsed her mouth and blotted her face with a wet paper towel, then found a chair and sank into it. Judy was blocking the door with another chair.

By that time, someone was knocking.

Judy opened the door a crack. "It's just Mother and Sandy," she said, allowing them to squeeze inside. "Sandy, get out the antacid. Lucy's sick."

"You brought antacid to my wedding?" Lucy asked.

"We came prepared for any eventuality," Sandy said as she produced the pink stomach medicine. "How sick are you?"

"I should have eloped," Lucy grumbled before taking a swig right out of the bottle.

"Nonsense," said Gwen, who was doing her best to revive Lucy's squashed bouquet. "You're going to pull yourself together and get your caboose up to Judge Hadley's chambers."

She wanted to—she really, really wanted to gather up her strength and march straight to Travis. But it was as if some invisible cords bound her to that chair in the bathroom. The crowd outside the door embodied her worst nightmare.

"I can't face those people," she said in a small voice. "What if I go out there and I faint, or get sick again?"

"We'll be with you, sweetheart," Gwen said soothingly.

"I have a better idea," said Lucy, fixing her mother with a hopeful look. "Let's bring Judge Hadley and Travis down here."

Gwen stiffened visibly. "I've been more than flexible about the informality of this ceremony," she said, "but I will not stand by and let my daughter be married in a public rest room. That's final."

"Oh, I suppose you're right," Lucy said with a sigh. "It wouldn't reflect very well on Travis."

Sandy unwrapped some soda crackers and gave
them to Lucy. "Here, these will help settle your
stomach. You are going through with it, aren't
you?"

"I...yes, of course. Just give me some time to get
used to the idea of facing that crowd, okay?"

Gwen looked infinitely relieved. "I'll go find
Travis and explain the delay. Five minutes?" she
asked Lucy optimistically.

"Better make it ten."

Gwen started to squeeze out the door, then
paused for a parting shot. "Judy, Sandy, don't
leave her alone for a minute. I don't like the way she
keeps looking at that window."

Travis paced Judge Hadley's chambers—back
and forth, back and forth. "Where is she?" he demanded of no one in particular. "She's five minutes late."

"Relax, Travis," said Nan, looking unusually
elegant in a flowing navy blue dress, her hair pinned
neatly into a bun. "The way you've been acting this
morning, it's obvious Lucy's not the only one with
frazzled nerves. I can't wait to tell her that you tried
to brush your teeth with shaving cream."

"They probably couldn't find a place to park,"
added his mother. She sat primly next to his father
on a dainty love seat, unable to mask her disapproval. She still hadn't reckoned with the fact that

her only son was marrying a woman she'd never met.

Judge Richard Hadley, an old friend of the Walkers, stood uneasily behind his desk polishing his wire-rimmed glasses. "Mr. Blakeman, I'm so sorry. I had no idea publicity was such an enormous concern or I would have kept the ceremony a secret."

"At least it wasn't me who blabbed this time," Nan said cheerfully.

A strident knock sent Travis flying to the door. He opened it with an audible whoosh of relief, until he realized that the somber little party filing in didn't include Lucy—just Gwen and Leon and the two brothers-in-law.

"Where is she?" he demanded again, a little more curtly than he intended.

"Well, now, Travis," Gwen began diplomatically, "there's been a little delay but everything's fine. She'll be here in about ten minutes."

"Why? What happened?"

"Just a small touch of bridal jitters, nothing to worry about—"

"Nothing to worry about!" he exploded. "Last time she had bridal jitters she jumped out a window!" Willing himself to calm down, he leaned his forearm against the wall and rested his head against it for a moment until he mastered his temper.

"Where is she?" he asked one more time, though he softened his tone.

Leon put a fatherly arm around Travis's shoulders and drew him aside. "You know how women are sometimes. She's just freshening up in the powder room downstairs—"

Travis didn't wait to hear more. He had to see her. He broke free of Leon's grasp and made for the door. He exited the judge's chambers before anyone could stop him.

His passage downstairs didn't go unnoticed, of course. With the accuracy of heat-seeking missiles the reporters found him and dogged his steps across the rotunda, but he didn't stop to talk. A SWAT team couldn't have slowed his progress. They watched in fascinated awe as he barged into the ladies' rest room with the force of a tornado, sending the chair that had been blocking the door sliding and bumping across the tile floor.

"Lucy, are you in here?" he boomed, but in the next second he saw her. She'd been standing at the sink doing something with her makeup, and at his noisy entrance she'd spun to face him, dropping a lipstick. She looked pale and tense and still utterly, utterly beautiful.

She was so shocked to see him, looking big and angry and incongruously male in the pink-tiled ladies' room, that she said the first thing that entered her head. "New suit?"

He didn't answer, but he gave each of her sisters a quelling look that sent them scurrying unquestioningly for the exit.

"See ya, Luce," Judy said over her shoulder as they tumbled out the door. "We'll be waiting for you."

"Travis, what are you doing here?" she finally asked.

"I might ask you the same thing," he countered. "You were supposed to be in Judge Hadley's chambers ten minutes ago."

"I was coming. I was," she insisted when he raised a dubious eyebrow. "It's just that I ... got sick."

"Sick?" His ire melted in the face of his obvious concern. "You didn't faint again, did you?"

"No. But the butterflies in my stomach got ugly," she clarified. "I had to make sure I was all right before I came out again in front of all those ... people."

"How do you feel now?"

"Better," she answered, not too convincingly.

His manner softened immeasurably. "You look beautiful. I mean it," he insisted when she started to deny it. "They say all brides are beautiful, but you look like an angel."

Her flush of embarrassment chased away the last of her pallor. "You weren't supposed to see me before the ceremony," she said. "It's bad luck for the groom to see the bride—"

"Are you my bride?" he asked suddenly, his eyes burning with intensity. "Are you going through with it?"

"Yes! Oh, Travis, believe me, it was never my intention to back out of marrying you. I even suggested bringing you and Judge Hadley down here, but Mother threw a fit." She wandered over to the bathroom's lone window and stared out through the frosted glass. "It's just that ... Are you sure you don't want to escape with me and elope to Reno?"

He shook his head adamantly and crooked his finger at her. "Come here," he said in a tone of voice that could not be ignored. "Give me your hand."

She hesitated. She knew that when she did what he asked, there would be no more delaying, no changing her mind. But when she looked up into those whiskey-brown eyes, so full of love and compassion, she found it easy to trust him—with her life, if it ever came to that. She held out her hand and offered him a tremulous smile. He smiled back, wrapping her hand securely in his, and suddenly she wasn't afraid anymore.

A fractured cheer went up from the onlookers as Travis and Lucy emerged from the ladies' room hand in hand. But Lucy didn't think about the crowd, or all those eyes fixed on her, or the flashes from photographers' cameras. She clutched at Travis's hand like an anchor and stared at the path ahead of her, concentrating only on placing one foot in front of the other.

Before she knew it they were in Judge Hadley's chambers. Lucy had requested a short ceremony and Judge Hadley obliged. She repeated her vows in a surprisingly strong voice while Travis, her rock, her pillar of strength, stumbled over the words like a schoolboy who hadn't studied his lessons. But together they got the job done; he slipped a plain gold band on her finger and suddenly the judge was pronouncing them husband and wife.

Travis took both her hands and looked at her expectantly, his eyes dancing with mischief. Lucy realized with a start that he was going to kiss her in front of all these people. She closed her eyes and surrendered to it, not caring in the least.

He kissed her briefly but tenderly, then held her close and whispered, "You did it."

"I did, didn't I."

They were plucked apart to endure hugs and kisses of congratulations, but soon they found each other again. They held hands, twining fingers and staring at each other giddily, and suddenly all Lucy could think about was getting him alone and showing him just how much she loved him, this man who had been willing to give up so much for her.

Her stomach picked that moment to rumble ominously, but it was only a healthy sign of hunger, not the horrible nervous jitters that had plagued her earlier.

"I'm starving," she announced as she plucked the hated hat from her head. "Which way to the food?" She started for the door, but Travis stopped her.

"Wait a minute, what about all those people?"

She paused, a little shocked that she'd forgotten so quickly about the crowd downstairs.

Judge Hadley cleared his throat. "I think I have a solution to the problem," he said, moving toward another door unobtrusively disguised with a potted ficus. "This leads to a fire escape that takes you to the staff parking lot. My car is out there. I'll drive Lucy and Travis to the house myself."

"Thank you, Richard, that's very kind," said Leon as he helped the judge move the plant.

"No, wait."

Everyone in the room went very still and stared at Lucy, who had spoken up so unexpectedly.

"What is it, dear?" Gwen prompted.

"I don't want to sneak out the back. I'm going to face them."

There were several audible gasps. Travis's mouth dropped open.

"Oh, dear," Leon mumbled.

"As the mayor's wife, I'll have certain civic responsibilities, and ducking the press isn't one of them." Now that the wedding was behind her, she was filled with a certain reckless abandon. She could do anything with Travis by her side, holding her hand. He would never let anything bad happen to her.

"That's fine, darling," Travis said, "but you don't have to start today."

But she was already reaching for the door. "Yes, I do. I have to start when I'm feeling brave, and I've never felt braver than right this moment."

She led him out of the chambers, down the hall and down the staircase to the accompaniment of applause and a few wolf whistles. She didn't pause until she was right in the middle of the crowd, even when the television lights beamed into her eyes.

The ever-vigilant reporter went for Travis first, teeth flashing. "So, Mr. Blakeman, is it official now? Are you and Ms. Walker married?"

"Yes," he replied. Then he just stood there grinning.

Lucy squeezed his hand in what had to be a painfully tight grip. *Talk, Travis,* she wanted to say. *This is free publicity.*

The reporter shifted to her. "Ms. Walker," he began.

"Mrs. B-Blakeman," she corrected him, hearing the hated stutter and the thin, wishy-washy voice and wishing she could evaporate on the spot. God, whose dumb idea was this? But it was too late to back out now.

They stood there for ten grueling minutes. Travis limited himself to one-word answers. Lucy got all the difficult questions. Somehow she stumbled and stuttered and blushed her way through them. Her words got all mixed up, and several things she said drew laughter when they weren't supposed to, but always she managed to correct herself and get the right message across.

At last Leon came to their rescue, interrupting the interview to announce that their car was out front. "The wedding cake will get stale if you stand here much longer," he added.

"Wait," one of the photographers shouted, "can't we get a kiss for the camera?"

"No!" Lucy said at once, just as Travis said, "Okay." She was overruled, and found herself swept up into a *Gone With the Wind* style kiss that elicited a final round of applause.

"And I thought you weren't playing up to the press," she grumbled as they at last made their escape.

To her surprise there was a gorgeous silver limousine waiting for them. "I didn't order this," she said as the chauffeur opened the door for her.

"Compliments of my parents," said Travis, sliding in after her. "They wanted to do something."

"Well, how nice!" How *very* nice, she added mentally when she realized they would be quite alone for a few minutes, secure in a tinted-glass co-coon. "Care to give a repeat performance of that kiss back there to a private audience?" she asked as soon as the door closed.

He pulled her close and nuzzled her hair. "Mmm, don't get me started. We might find ourselves skipping the reception and heading straight for the Hide-Away Lodge. Oh, Lucy, you were terrific back there."

"I was a babbling, stuttering idiot and you know it," she corrected him, although at that moment she really didn't care.

"You had everyone in that courthouse eating out of your hand," he insisted. "I was so proud of you. My heart was so full I couldn't breathe—in fact, I'm the one who couldn't wedge two consecutive words out of my throat."

*He was proud of her.* God, that made it all worthwhile. She felt suddenly filled with purpose, dedication and inspiration. "Travis Blakeman, I'm going to be the best damn politician's wife that ever walked this earth. I'm going to work at it—you'll see. I'll practice in front of the mirror. I'll get my mother's recipes and learn how to entertain—"

He did kiss her then, stealing away every coherent thought in her head, and for the next ten minutes they both became blissfully forgetful of politics.

# Epilogue

Lucy's hand was beginning to cramp, but it never occurred to her to loosen her grip. For hour after hour now, sitting in a noisy hotel suite at the River Inn, she'd held Travis's hand as they waited for the election results. The suite was filled with balloons, silly hats, noisemakers and half-eaten trays of hors d'oeuvres, but the atmosphere was far from party-like. The race was too close for comfort.

Travis was nervous. He'd already knocked over two cups of coffee and had resumed biting his fingernails, a habit he'd given up at age ten. For once, Lucy found herself in the odd position of being the calm one, the one offering soothing words of reassurance.

A hush fell over the room as the latest poll results were announced; though Travis had held the lead for most of the evening, Wendall Cox had just pulled ahead by a tiny margin.

Travis tried to look like it didn't matter, but Lucy knew better. "I have this terrible feeling I'm not going to lose gracefully," he whispered into her ear.

"You're not going to lose at all," she whispered back, reaching up to ruffle his hair, already unruly from Travis running nervous fingers through it uncounted times.

Leon sat next to Travis to offer his observations. "It's just a blip, son," he said with a reassuring thump on his son-in-law's shoulder. "Why, it wouldn't be a horse race if you ran away with it."

"I don't want a horse race," Travis argued with less than his usual good sportsmanship. "I want to win." His grip on Lucy's hand tightened unconsciously. She winced and gamely said nothing.

"How are you holding up?" It was Gwen, placing a comforting arm around Lucy's shoulders.

"Better than I expected," Lucy responded with a sideways glance at Travis. "I got through an interview without stuttering once. He's the one who's ready for a straitjacket."

"I seem to remember that your father didn't handle his first election night well, either," said Gwen. "I had to keep him dosed up with antacid."

Lucy couldn't help it; she laughed. "I knew I inherited that trait from someone."

. Just after midnight, Travis's campaign manager stood on a chair to make an announcement. An expectant hush fell over the room as Marty cleared his throat and assumed a grave expression. "I just received a call from the election commissioner," he said calmly. "All the votes have been tallied and the results confirmed." He paused dramatically. "The annexation issue passed by a narrow margin." A smattering of applause greeted that statement, but that wasn't what people wanted to hear.

"As for the mayor's race," he continued, then paused again, pursing his lips. Lucy was sure her finger bones were going to be crushed in Travis's grip before Marty, in an utterly deadpan voice, finally spit out the results. "Travis won."

The room exploded with cheering as Travis sprang out of his chair, carrying Lucy with him and wrapping her in an exuberant hug. She wiggled her fingers to renew circulation to them, then gave Travis a quick kiss. "Good job," she said, wishing she could think of more adequate words.

"Thanks," he acknowledged. "Now you don't have to shoot me."

Champagne corks popped and toasts were offered, but Lucy didn't need any bubbly. She was flying high on victory, not to mention the prospect of having her husband home with her on a regular basis. For the past two months they'd passed like ships in the night—affectionate ships, to be sure, but also exhausted ones. She couldn't wait to experience the full array of what their marriage could embrace—weekend barbecues with friends, quiet nights in front of the fireplace, lazy Sunday mornings with just themselves and the newspaper for company.

"You have a funny look on your face," Travis said when there was a pause in the rowdy congratulations.

"Just looking forward to the future," she admitted. "I'm glad all this election nonsense is over, aren't you?"

He quirked an eyebrow at her. "I don't know," he said, shifting her so that he could put his hands around her tiny waist. "I could get used to all this attention."

"How about some attention from me?" she countered, sliding her arms around his neck. "I'll bet you could get used to that."

He smiled wickedly. "What a novel idea. What do you say we get out of here?"

"Marvelous suggestion."

Making an escape wasn't easy. Though they were tempted to slip away unnoticed, Lucy reminded Travis that it wouldn't be very polite to all the volunteers who had given so freely of their time and energy. So they announced their leave-taking, and consequently it was another thirty minutes before they made it out the door.

The cold November air was bracing. Once sequestered in the privacy of Travis's Fiat, Lucy dropped her guard and gave him a congratulatory kiss—not the little peck she'd given him earlier, for the public eye, but the one he deserved, the one that encompassed all her love and pride.

"Mmm," he said, nuzzling her ear, "we might not ever make it out of the parking lot at this rate."

"Oh, yes, we will. Bucket seats simply will not accommodate all that I have in mind."

That prompted him to start the engine.

Lucy leaned back in drowsy contentment as Travis drove them home. Soon, however, she noticed they were heading the wrong way. "I know it's late, Travis, and I'm awfully tired, but don't we live *that* way?" She pointed behind them.

"Not anymore."

"What are you talking about?"

But he merely gave her an enigmatic smile and continued on an unerring path to some mysterious destination.

A short time later he turned onto Highway 7, which meandered its way into the hills north of town, and Lucy began to suspect.

"You didn't!" she said as he turned into the driveway of the gingerbread house, the very home they had discussed on the day they met. "You didn't really buy this house, did you?"

He pulled around to the back of the house and into a narrow carport. "Not exactly. Come on, you'll see."

She didn't wait for another invitation, but sprang out of the car and followed Travis like an eager puppy to the front door. He put the key in the lock and opened the door with an air of familiarity, then swept Lucy into his arms and carried her over the threshold.

The moment he set her down, she knew that the house belonged to him. Every picture on the wall, every stick of the polished antique furniture, every rug screamed his name. His attractive but rather sterile town house had never done that. "You did buy it," she whispered in awe.

"No. It's always been mine. My grandmother left it to me. The problem was, if I wanted to be mayor of Brennerton I had to live within the city limits."

Lucy's face fell. "Then you still can't really live here."

He gave her a cagey smile. "Oh, yes, I can—since the annexation issue passed, this house is officially part of Brennerton. Welcome home, Lucy."

For a few moments she couldn't say anything, she was so overwhelmed.

"You do want to live here, don't you?" he asked uncertainly. "I mean, it's not too far from town, is it? And you can get that puppy you've been talking about—and a cat and geese and even a pony—"

She effectively cut him off by launching herself into his arms. "Oh, Travis, it's perfect—just perfect. Is the whole house full of antiques?"

"Every room. I think you'll especially like the oak four-poster in the master bedroom..."

She gave him a throaty laugh. "If that's not a politician for you. Always an angle." Still, she allowed him to take her hand and lead her unresisting to the room in question.

\*　\*　\*　\*　\*

**HARLEQUIN®**

Don't miss these Harlequin favorites by some of our most distinguished authors!
And now, you can receive a discount by ordering two or more titles!

| | | |
|---|---|---|
| HT #25663 | THE LAWMAN<br>by Vicki Lewis Thompson | $3.25 U.S.☐/$3.75 CAN. ☐ |
| HP #11788 | THE SISTER SWAP<br>by Susan Napier | $3.25 U.S.☐/$3.75 CAN. ☐ |
| HR #03293 | THE MAN WHO CAME FOR CHRISTMAS<br>by Bethany Campbell | $2.99 U.S.☐/$3.50 CAN. ☐ |
| HS #70667 | FATHERS & OTHER STRANGERS<br>by Evelyn Crowe | $3.75 U.S.☐/$4.25 CAN. ☐ |
| HI #22198 | MURDER BY THE BOOK<br>by Margaret St. George | $2.89 ☐ |
| HAR #16520 | THE ADVENTURESS<br>by M.J. Rodgers | $3.50 U.S.☐/$3.99 CAN. ☐ |
| HH #28885 | DESERT ROGUE<br>by Erin Yorke | $4.50 U.S.☐/$4.99 CAN. ☐ |

**(limited quantities available on certain titles)**

| | | |
|---|---|---|
| | AMOUNT | $ |
| DEDUCT: | 10% DISCOUNT FOR 2+ BOOKS | $ |
| ADD: | POSTAGE & HANDLING | $ |
| | ($1.00 for one book, 50¢ for each additional) | |
| | APPLICABLE TAXES** | $_____ |
| | **TOTAL PAYABLE** | $_____ |
| | (check or money order—please do not send cash) | |

To order, complete this form and send it, along with a check or money order for the total above, payable to Harlequin Books, to: **In the U.S.:** 3010 Walden Avenue, P.O. Box 9047, Buffalo, NY 14269-9047; **In Canada:** P.O. Box 613, Fort Erie, Ontario, L2A 5X3.

Name:_____

Address:_____ City:_____

State/Prov.:_____ Zip/Postal Code:_____

**New York residents remit applicable sales taxes.
Canadian residents remit applicable GST and provincial taxes.

HBACK-JS3

Look us up on-line at: http://www.romance.net

**_Harlequin Romance_** ®

**D**elightful

**A**ffectionate

**R**omantic

**E**motional

**T**ender

**O**riginal

**D**aring

**R**iveting

**E**nchanting

**A**dventurous

**M**oving

Harlequin Romance—the
series that has it all!

HROM-G

# HARLEQUIN 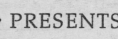 PRESENTS®

**HARLEQUIN PRESENTS**
men you won't be able to resist falling in love with...

**HARLEQUIN PRESENTS**
women who have feelings just like your own...

**HARLEQUIN PRESENTS**
powerful passion in exotic international settings...

**HARLEQUIN PRESENTS**
intense, dramatic stories that will keep you turning
to the very last page...

**HARLEQUIN PRESENTS**
The world's bestselling romance series!

# ◆ Harlequin®
## ® Historical

If you're a serious fan of historical romance,
then you're in luck!

Harlequin Historicals brings you
stories by bestselling authors, rising new stars
and talented first-timers.

Ruth Langan & Theresa Michaels
Mary McBride & Cheryl St. John
Margaret Moore & Merline Lovelace
Julie Tetel & Nina Beaumont
Susan Amarillas & Ana Seymour
Deborah Simmons & Linda Castle
Cassandra Austin & Emily French
Miranda Jarrett & Suzanne Barclay
DeLoras Scott & Laurie Grant...

You'll never run out of favorites.

Harlequin Historicals...they're too good to miss!

# HARLEQUIN®
## I N T R I G U E ®

# THAT'S INTRIGUE—DYNAMIC ROMANCE AT ITS BEST!

Harlequin Intrigue is now bringing you more—more men and mystery, more desire and danger. If you've been looking for thrilling tales of contemporary passion and sensuous love stories with taut, edge-of-the-seat suspense—then you'll *love* Harlequin Intrigue!

Every month, you'll meet four new heroes who are guaranteed to make your spine tingle and your pulse pound. With them you'll enter into the exciting world of Harlequin Intrigue—where your life is on the line and so is your heart!

**Harlequin Intrigue—we'll leave you breathless!**

## LOOK FOR OUR FOUR FABULOUS MEN!

Each month some of today's bestselling authors bring four new fabulous men to Harlequin American Romance. Whether they're rebel ranchers, millionaire power brokers or sexy single dads, they're all gallant princes—and they're all ready to sweep you into lighthearted fantasies and contemporary fairy tales where anything is possible and where all your dreams come true!

You don't even have to make a wish...Harlequin American Romance will grant your every desire!

Look for Harlequin American Romance wherever Harlequin books are sold!

## WAYS TO UNEXPECTEDLY MEET MR. RIGHT:

♡ Go out with the sexy-sounding stranger your daughter secretly set you up with through a personal ad.

♡ RSVP yes to a wedding invitation—soon it might be your turn to say "I do!"

♡ Receive a marriage proposal by mail— from a man you've never met....

These are just a few of the unexpected ways that written communication leads to love in Silhouette Yours Truly.

Each month, look for two fast-paced, fun and flirtatious Yours Truly novels (with entertaining treats and sneak previews in the back pages) by some of your favorite authors—and some who are sure to become favorites.

## YOURS TRULY™:
Love—when you least expect it!

# George Hamilton
## and
## Alana Collins

George Hamilton—he of the deepest tan—married Alana Collins in 1972. Only three friends and Alana's dog attended the wedding ceremony held atop the Hilton Hotel in Las Vegas. Both bride and groom wore love beads and blue jeans.

In 1974, the couple had a son, Ashley. He was later briefly married to actress Shannon Doherty.

George and Alana Hamilton's marriage ended in divorce in 1976.

B-GEORGE